Milton Nobles

Love and Law

An Original Comedy-drama in Four Acts

Milton Nobles

Love and Law
An Original Comedy-drama in Four Acts

ISBN/EAN: 9783744787796

Printed in Europe, USA, Canada, Australia, Japan

Cover: Foto ©Andreas Hilbeck / pixelio.de

More available books at **www.hansebooks.com**

AN ORIGINAL COMEDY-DRAMA IN FOUR ACTS.

BY

MILTON NOBLES.

Entered according to Act of Congress, in the Librarian's Office, at Washington, D. C ,
in the year 1883, by
MILTON NOBLES,

PHILADELPHIA :

LEDGER JOB PRINT.

1884.

LOVE AND LAW.

A COMEDY-DRAMA IN FOUR ACTS,

BY

ᗰILTON ᑎOBLES.

ORIGINAL CAST.

RITTA, an Italian Street Singer, ... DOLLIE NOBLES
HELEN MONTAGUE, an English Lady of wealth, ... AGNES HERNDON
MRS. TARBOX, Mistress of Bay View Cottage, ... FLORENCE VINCENT
KITTY O'ROURKE, servant to Mrs. Tarbox, ... JENNIE SATTERLEE
OLD ROSA, an Italian Crone, companion to Conti, ... JENNIE CARROLL
Lady Guests at Bay View Cottage.

SIR RANDALL BURNS, Bart . . . . MYRON W. LEFFINGWELL
JASPER CRADDOCK, the Black Sheep of a wealthy English family, . . O. H. BARR
SEPTIMUS SAWYER, Attorney-at-Law, New York City, . . . BENJ. G ROGERS
JIMMIE NIPPER, alias "Cockney Jim," a London Thief, . . . HARRY RAINFORTH
GIOVANNI CONTI, an Italian Organ Grinder, ... GEORGE W. BARNUM
FERDINAND HOFFMEIER, "One of the Finest," . . . . MAX FEHRMANN
THEOPHILUS CRANE, Clerk to Sawyer, ... EDWIN L. MORTIMER
THE "DUDE" BOARDER, ... WILLIE B. WRIGHT
THE GROCER'S MAN, ... B. A. LONG
THE BUTCHER'S MAN, ... WILL B THAYER
JOSEPH SKERRETT, an English Detective Officer, ... F. I. KETCHUM
FELIX O'PAFF, Attorney-at-Law, New York City, (late of Dublin,) MILTON NOBLES
Gentlemen guests at Bay View Cottage.

SYNOPSIS OF THE SCENERY AND INCIDENTS.

ACT I —LOVE—The Intimation. Scene—Bay View Cottage, Staten Island, with a view of New York Bay and Harbor. (Hoyt & Brother.)

ACT II.—LOVE—The Inspiration. Scene—The Den of Giovanni Conti, Crosby Street, New York City. (Thomas Plaisted)

ACT III.—LOVE—The Realization Scene—The Boudoir of Helen Montague, New York City. (Hoyt & Brother.)

ACT IV.—LAW—The Consummation. Scene 1.—Law Office of Sawyer and O'Paff. Scene 2—A street adjoining the residence of Helen Montague. Scene 3.—The Den of Giovanni Conti.

A lapse of Ten Hours between the First and Second Acts. A lapse of Eight Months between the Second and Third Acts. A lapse of Four Weeks between the Third and Fourth Acts.

First produced at the Corinthian Academy of Music, Rochester, N.Y., April 17th, 1884. Fourteenth Street Theatre, New York City, April 21st, 1884.

LOVE AND LAW,

AN ORIGINAL COMEDY-DRAMA

BY

MILTON NOBLES.

———— ◆ ————

ACT I.

*Bay View Cottage,. Staten Island, over-looking New York
Bay and Harbor, handsome set house R., extending up
from first grooves. Practical balcony above, door opening
on balcony, veranda below, slightly elevated gauze window, exposing interior of Cottage to audience. Balcony
ornamented with hanging baskets and climbing vines, etc.,
etc. Bay seen as from an elevation, small profile boats,
steam and sail, passing during entire act. Ornamental
picket fence at back, crossing stage. Open gate in C., large
tree set L 2., circular seat around tree, hammock swung
between two trees L. 3 E., rustic tables R. and L., rustic
chairs, etc., etc. Swing at back R.*

*Lights all up, lively music at rise, guests discovered on upper
balcony, one on lower porch, gent in hammock, lady reading
to him. Colored porter enters at back, followed by boy, both
loaded down with marketing, they pass into house R. as*
SAWYER *comes out.*

SEPTIMUS SAWYER, *a hale and hearty middle-aged lawyer,
with morning papers in hand,* X. *to seat* L.

Sawyer. It looks as though we were going to have a
square meal for dinner to-day.   [*Sits* L.
    [*Guests gradually saunter off. Gent and lady at ham-
mock exit* C.
    I hope I shall be allowed ten minutes quiet here, I can't
get it in the house; if ever I envied Robinson Crusoe his

(3)

solitude, it has been during my visit to this alleged " quiet retreat." I'm fond of music, and I like children, but even " Monastery Bells " and the " Mulligan Guards " pall on one, when compelled to listen to them morning, noon and night, ground out of an old family relic of a cracked piano, by a ten year old "infant phenomenon." I'll see if I can't get time to look over the markets and court reports. [*reads.* " Supreme court decisions, case 421, verdict of lower court affirmed." Good.

Enter NICHOLAS CRANE, *clerk to* SAWYER, *a middle-aged old fellow, eccentric in make up, through gate at back, he has a green bag filled with briefs.*

Crane. Good morning, Mr. Sawyer.   [*Down* C.

Sawyer. Ah, Mr. Crane, good morning, what brings you up here?

Crane. Business, sir; Business, sir: In the service of our noble profession the law.

Sawyer. Yes, yes, I've heard that before. What is it?

Crane. Documents: Buncombe *vs.* Biesley. Mr. S. said it was necessary that you examine them to-day.

Sawyer. Of course, that's his idea of a vacation is it? All right, have you breakfasted?

Crane. No, sir, up and doing always. Business first and always, is my motto, in the pursuit of our noble profession the law.

Sawyer. You're too zealous Crane, go into the house, they will get you some breakfast, take the papers with you, and leave them in the office.

Crane. Yes, sir; I will sir; even the greatest of us must eat, it is a duty we owe to society, food stimulates the stomach, the stomach stimulates the brain, the brain formulates the law, and the law governs the world.

[*Exit* CRANE *into house* R.

Sawyer. [*Reading*], Case 360 verdict set aside and a new trial ordered. Ha, ha, well that is good.

[*Enter from house* MRS. TARBOX.

Mrs. Tarbox. Good morning, Mr. Sawyer, anything new in the papers?

Sawyer. Haven't had time to look. I've just been glancing over the court reports and markets.

Mrs. Tarbox. Aint they terrible?

Sawyer. What?

Mrs. Tarbox. Why the markets, butter fifty cents a pound, eggs forty cents a dozen, its terrible.

Sawyer. I was not referring to the provisions but to the money market, bonds and stocks.

Mrs. Tarbox. Oh yes, of course; when poor dear Henry was alive he was the same; he always wore one.

Sawyer. Wore what?

Mrs. Tarbox. Stocks.

Sawyer. [*Aside.*] This old woman is a nuisance. [*Aloud.*] I think I'll take a stroll. Please be kind enough to tell Kitty to bring my claret and biscuit out here, and when I return I'll take my luncheon.

Mrs. Tarbox. [*Going to house.*] Certainly, Mr. Sawyer, I'll have the claret put on ice at once.

[*Exit* MRS. TARBOX *into house* R.

Sawyer. 'Tis no wonder that "poor dear Henry" is dead. What a blessed relief he must have found in "shuffling off." I'll go down to the inlet and anchor myself off in a boat, and see if I can read my paper in peace and quiet there.

[*Exit* SAWYER, L. I E.

Enter at back HELEN MONTAGUE *and* SIR RANDALL BURNS, *they approach house,* HELEN *offers her hand,* SIR RANDALL BURNS *takes it and retaining it, speaks.*

Sir Randall Burns. One moment Helen, do not leave me thus, let me finish now.

Helen Montague. Sir Randall why dwell further upon the subject? It but inflicts needless pain.

Sir Randall. Helen I would die sooner than cause you one moment of pain, but I must know upon what grounds your refusal of my suit is based; sit here for a moment. [*She hesitates.*] Surely you can grant that trifling request?

Helen. [*Aside, dropping into seat by tree.*] I cannot spare myself one moment of pain. [SIR RANDALL *sits beside her.*

Sir Randall. Helen, three years ago, in England, I paid to you such attentions as a man pays only to the woman he honestly loves. I did not then plainly speak of my affection, for my circumstances were not such as to warrant me in proposing for the hand of the rich heiress, the idol of our circle, but you knew, all knew, that I loved you. Is it not so?

Helen. [*With downcast head.*] Yes, Sir Randall, I knew it.

Sir Randall. Once, and once only, did I allow my feelings to get the better of my judgment, I do not know what I said, my words were broken, but they were words of love, and I thought Helen; heaven help me if hope led me to error, but I thought that in that moment of joy, I recognized a something in your sad sweet face which told me that some time I might speak, and not fear your answer.

Helen. Sir Randall, I beg you to spare me further recital of that scene.

Sir Randall. A few words more and I am silent, I was called to Scotland by the death of a relative, who left me a princely fortune, when I returned rich, and in a position to declare myself, I found that you had gone, where, no one could tell. Selling my commission in the army, I came to America in search of forgetfulness, chance or a blessed fatality again brought us face to face; but still you are sad and thoughtful, refusing both confidence and consolation. Tell me Helen, what is the cause?

Helen. Do not ask me, I cannot speak, Sir Randall.

Sir Randall. Your reticence shall be respected Helen, only tell me frankly, can I, may I hope?

Helen. Sir Randall, for the present at least, there is no hope that I can offer.

Sir Randall. I thank you for your forbearance in permitting my attentions, I hope at least to be considered a friend.

Helen. [*Aside.*] Could I but speak. [*Aloud.*] Yes, as a very, very, dear friend.   [*Giving him her hand.*

Sir Randall. [*Taking her hand.*] Even for that I am thankful.

Enter KITTY *from house, with bottle of claret, glasses and plate of biscuit,* SIR RANDALL *and* HELEN *quickly separate,* KITTY X'S L., *and puts tray on table.*

Sir Randall. [*In lively tones.*] Remember, Mrs. Montague you promised to back your ponies against my grays for a dozen of gloves.

Helen. [*Gaily.*] And I shall win them too, remember twelve buttons.

Sir Randall. Oh, I have the size and make.

Helen. This afternoon at four on the shore road.

Sir Randall. I will be on hand, until then adieu.

Helen. Adieu, Sir Randall.

[*Exit* HELEN *in house* R., *exit* SIR RANDALL *through gate* C., *and off.*

Kitty. [*Who has been observing them.*] Aha, that's a foine way them illigant folks have of saying phat they don't mane, there's more than you kin see wid looking at 'em. A foine illigant couple they'd make, he's a rale lord, he's a rale gintleman too, I can tell that by his always giving me fifty cents whin I wait on him; and she's a foine lady, an a widdy too. Oh, dear, but there's something about thim widdy's thet bothers the min entirely. There Mr. Sawyer, there's your lunch Oh, he's a great lawyer, is Mr. Sawyer, as sits all day on a high binch and sez "are ye guilty or are yez not guilty."

[*Enter at back* FERDINAND HOFFMEIER, *a New York police-man, in undress uniform.*

Hoffmeier. [*At back, over fence.*] Hello! Kitty! How was the queen of hearts?

Kitty. Och, there's Mr. Hoffmeier. [*Curtsies.*] Good morning, Mr. Hoffmeier.

Hoffmeier. Goot morning. [*Coming down* C] How you vas to-day?

Kitty. Very well, I tank you sur. Have ye any news for me to-day?

Hoffmeier. I've got more dan news. I've got de col-lateral.

Kitty. Phats that?

Hoffmeier. I've got your vatch, und your rings, und your money. [*Producing articles.*]

Kitty. Oh, Mother of Moses! An' have I got them all back again?

Hoffmeier. Everyding. [*Giving them.*]

Kitty. The blessing of St. Patrick upon you Mr. Hoff-meier.

Hoffmeier. Call me Ferdinand, dots my front name.

Kitty. Well, Ferdinand, I'll thank you, an' pray for ye ivery day of my life. How much is to pay?

Hoffmeier. Don't thank me, und dere's nodings to pay. Besides, it wasn't me gott de dings back, anyway.

Kitty. Wasn't it. Well who was it?

Hoffmeier. It vas dot coundryman of yours. Dot lawyer, Mr. O'Paff. He sawn dem swindlers ven dey vos hanging around Castle Garden, robbing de emmigrants, und ven dey gott holt of you, he followed dem, und gott me to help him mit de case.

Kitty. Heavens bliss him.   That was my mother's wedding ring, an' the watch has been in the family a hundred years.

Hoffmeier. Vell I should dink so by de looks of it.   Mr. O'Paff gott de fellers send oop for two years, und den dere vas some trouble godden de dings again back.   You see ve have lots of ret dape in the law bisness oud.

Kitty. Yis, I suppose so.

Hoffmeier. Bud you got everyding back at last now.   De money vas ten dollars short, but Mr. O'Paff made dot up himself; so you have got everyding yust as you lost it.

Kitty. Oh, he's a foine man.   An' he wouldn't take any pay ?

Hoffmeier. Nod a cend.

Kitty. Oh, this is a great country.

Hoffmeier. You bed your boods it's a great coundry, und de next dime vot you emigrate, you yust tooken your money und your vatches und dings, und sew dem up in your stocking in.

Kitty. Oh, Mr. Hoffmeier.

Hoffmeier. Now, Kiddy, dot everyding is settled, vot do you dink about settling down yourself.   How vould you like to join de force ?

Kitty. Well, Mr. Hoffmeier, I'm very thankful to you for all your kindness; but I'm a little onaisy about policemen. Phen I was workin fer Mrs. Col. O'Mulligan, at Bowling Green, in Dublin, there was a policeman who did his tryin' to coort me there, an' tellin' me quare yarns about his bein' dicinded from the Kings and Jukes of Ireland; an' that he would make me a Quane or a Jukess, an' the way that policeman would ate could vittals, an' make luve an' drink beer.   An' all the time he had a wife an' nine childer livin' in Tipperary.

Hoffmeier. Dot vos de same mit de Irish policeman here, dey vos a pad lot, look oud for dem.   But ven a Dutch policeman talks marry, you bed your boots he means pisness.

Kitty, But I haven't taken out me papers yit.

Hoffmeier. [*Putting his arm around her.*] I vill naduralize you mit de marriage certificate. [*Kisses her. Mrs. Tarbox appears in door of house.*]

Kitty. [*Nestling up to Hoffmeier,*] Is that the way you naturalize Dublin girls in this country?

Hoffmeier. Dots von of de vays.

Kitty. Well it's less trouble than I thought. You can naturalize me again if you have time. [*He is about to kiss her again when Mrs. Tarbox speaks.*]

Mrs. Tarbox. [*On porch of house.*] Young woman, if you think you are naturalized enough, you can come in and set the table for lunch. [*They separate at the sound of her voice.*]

Hoffmeier [*Importantly.*] Young vooman dit you see anyding of a black und dan dog around here. [*Whistles.*]

Kitty. Oh, murther! murther! [*Runs into house* R.

Hoffmeier. [*Whistling.*] Vere de tuyfel dit dot dog got to?

Mrs. Tarbox. I guess your dog has gone to get his naturalization papers.

Hoffmeier. Dot dog is here. I know it. He comes here every day ven de orchestra blays in de pavillion dere. He vos fond of music.

Mrs. Tarbox. A dog fond of music. How do you know he is?

Hoffmeier. Because he carries a brass band around his neck. [*Laughs at Mrs. Tarbox.*] Oh go und got naturalized.

Exit, laughing at MRS. TARBOX, *gate* R. C. MRS. TARBOX *flaunts angrily into house.*

Felix O'Paff. [*Off* L. U. E.] Aisy with that hat box, gently with that umbrella, my man. There you are, never mind the change. Buy a peck of oats with it, and give that old horse a square meal.

Music forte, Felix O'Paff enters L. C., *down, carries hat box, bag, umbrella, etc, etc.; well, but rather eccentrically dressed. A young, bright, good-looking fellow, with a touch of the brogue. Kitty comes from house.*

Kitty. Oh, a new arrival.

O'Paff. Well I'm here, but where am I? The place looked inviting and I tried it at a venture. [*Kitty comes down* C.] Excuse me young woman, but what is the name of this place?

Kitty. Is it the hotel yez mane?

O'Paff. House, grounds, demesne, and all the appurtenances thereto belonging. What do you call it, when you are under the necessity of giving it a name?

Kitty. Well sir, this Hotel is called the Bay View Cottage.

O'Paff. Full.

Kitty. Sur?

O'Paff. Are ye full?

Kitty. Is it the rooms ye mane sur?

O'Paff Did ye suppose I meant the boarders?

Kitty. Well, we're pretty well filled below sir, but there's some rooms up stairs.

O'Paff. Just like my profession. Crowded below, but plenty of room at the top. What are the names of some of your guests?

Kitty. Well, there's Mr. Sawyer sir, a great liyer in New York. Do you know him?

O'Paff. Well, there are so many great liars in New York. Is it Septimus Sawyer, the criminal lawyer you mean?

Kitty. That's the one sir. And thin there's a rale English Lord.

O'Paff. English Lord—some London cab-driver doing the grand, I suppose. Proceed Nora macushla.

Kitty. My name is not Nora, it's Kitty.

O'Paff. Kitty—Sweet Kathleen Mavourneen [*Sings it.*] And the ladies Kitty. If I have a strong weakness Kitty, it's for the ladies.

Kitty. There's a rich English widdy.

O'Paff. A widow?

Kitty. Young and beautiful.

O'Paff. [*Drops his bag on Kitty's feet.*] Oh; I beg pardon. [*Picks up bag.*] A beautiful widow. I'll anchor here. Where there is a young and pretty widow, there is where O'Paff flocks. I'll condole with her upon her recent loss. I suppose it is recent, Kitty?

Kitty. I don't know sur.

O'Paff. Well, we'll hope for the best. As a consoler of young widowhood, and a mitigator of lonely grief, I loom up.

Kitty. What name did you say sur?

O'Paff. [*Giving card.*] O'Paff, Felix O'Paff, Attorney-at-law, New York, late of Dublin.

Kitty. [*Falling on her knees and kissing O'Paff's hand.*] Oh, thin you're the kind gintleman who got back all of my money, and my mother's watch and wedding ring. Heaven bless you sir.

O'Paff. [*Looking at her.*] Why so it is my little Irish wayfarer that fell among thieves.

. *Kitty.* Oh, sir, never a night from that time to this, have I gone to me bed without mentioning you. And I hope you'll recave your reward in the nixt world, as you wouldn't take pay in this.

O'Paff. [*With feeling.*] Stand up child. In the course of a vagabond life, I have done many an act of kindness, often at the cost to myself of privation and self-denial, but I have never been repaid with gratitude so sincere as this.

Kitty. [*Crying.*] I was a stranger in a strange land.

O'Paff. Yes, dear, you were a stranger and they took you in. [*Puts his arm around her.*] Don't cry, dear, although my great specialty is widows, I am an expert in all branches of the female consolation line. [*Lays her head on his shoulder.*] Don't cry, dear. [*Wipes her eyes with handkerchief.* MRS. TARBOX *appears on veranda* R.]

Who ran to catch me when I fell,
And kissed the spot to make it well?

[*Kisses her.* MRS. TARBOX *coughs—examining* KITTY'S *tooth.*] Yes, young woman, it must come out or be filled. The molars being in immediate proximity to the incisors, demands prompt treatment. [MRS. TARBOX *coming down.*

Mrs. Tarbox. Kitty!

Kitty. [*Screams and runs up to door* R] Oh, murther!

Mrs. Tarbox. Are you getting another set of naturalization papers?

Kitty. [*Hand on her jaw.*] Oh, Doctor! Doctor!

[*Exit into house* R.

Mrs. Tarbox. Are you a dentist, sir?

O'Paff. [*Who has gathered up his traps.*] Not exactly Madam. I'm a lawyer. Yet it's but a step from Blackstone to Esculapius. While one puts a plaster on your back, the other applies a poultice to your pocketbook. [*Handing card to* MRS. TARBOX.]

Mrs. Tarbox. You're the second man I've caught kissing that young woman this morning. Kissing servant girls seems to be getting epidermic here·

O'Paff. Getting what, ma'am?

Mrs. Tarbox.. I said epidermic.

O'Paff. I wonder when that word was injected into the English language.   Is this a public house ma'am?

Mrs. Tarbox. [*Stiffly.*] It is sir.

O'Paff. [*Aside.*] I shall have to mollify the old lady. [*Aloud.*] Well Miss, could I see your father or mother?

Mrs. Tarbox. [*Simpering.*] Oh sir, I am the landlady.

O'Paff. [*Dropping bag on her foot.*] I beg your pardon. [*Picks up bag.*] I would'nt have thought it could be possible.

Mrs. Tarbox. And you're looking for a genteel retreat?

O'Paff. Exactly ; a temporary recreation, I'm completely run down with overwork, cutting off coupons, collecting interest, etc., etc.

Mrs. Tarbox. Yes, I know how it is.

O'Paff. [*Aside.*] I wish I did. [*Aloud.*] What are my chances ma'am?

Mrs. Tarbox. Well I'm pretty full. [*Pause.*] But I have a *sweet* of rooms on the top floor.

O'Paff. Rooms en suite eh?   Well I'm sure the rooms can be no more sweet and charming than the hostess.

Mrs. Tarbox. Really Mr. O'Paff.

O'Paff. I cannot flatter ma'am.

Mrs. Tarbox. You so remind me of poor, dear Henry.

O'Paff. I beg pardon but Henry is——?

Mrs. Tarbox. My late husband.   I am a widow.

O'Paff. [*Dropping bag on Mrs. Tarbox's foot.*] Oh, I beg your pardon. [*Aside.*] Another widow O'Paff ye divil, here is a vast field of usefulness.

Mrs. Tarbox. Henry was such a flatterer.   He used to call me " Little Goosey," and always declared that I was as beautiful as *Venice.*

O'Paff. He could'nt help it ma'am, the oracular proof was before him ; and like myself, he scorned to flatter.

Mrs. Tarbox. I dare say I was not unattractive then. But, I'm no longer a girl.

O'Paff. No ! still you were a girl once, there's a consolation in that.   You were a girl awhile ago, a *long* while ago.

Mrs. Tarbox. Sir !

O'Paff. Girlhood is but fleeting, youth is frivolous.   But the ripened charms and stately grace of a perfect womanhood, fills full the measure of –of–of–of mundane bliss.

Mrs. Tarbox. Now that I think of it, Mr. O'Paff, I have

a large room vacant on the second floor. It commands a
fine view of the bay.

O'Paff. Good, I'll take it.

Mrs. Tarbox. The terms will be——

O'Paff. Don't mention them my dear madam, must our
delightful conference, our feast of reason and flow of soul
be mingled with vulgar dross? If it were a hundred golden
golconda a week, with the happiness of your society it would
be cheap.

Mrs. Tarbox. [*Aside.*] He must be very wealthy.

O'Paff. [*Aside.*] I may as well give the old century plant
a good dose of taffy. I shall have nothing else to give her
until my quarterly allowance arrives from Dublin.

Mrs. Tarbox. I'll send the servant for your baggage.

O'Paff. Not at all ma'am, this satchel contains valuable
family jewels, and I prefer not to trust them out of my hands.

Mrs. Tarbox. Oh, very well. [*Going to house.*] We lunch
at twelve and dine at five.

O'Paff. I'll do your dinner justice ma'am. [*Exit Mrs.
Tarbox into house.*] Well that old woman can digest more
soft soap than a Chinese laundry. Let me see how the
family jewels are coming on. [*Sits on rustic seat* L. *of table,
opens bag.*] Six paper collars, one ditto bosom, four stockings, tooth brush, blacking ditto, Well it's lucky that old
woman did'nt insist upon examining my luggage. [*Sees wine
and biscuit on table.*] Hillo! here's a luncheon. Well now
that's thoughtful, [*Helps himself to wine, drinks.*] Not bad
either; try it again ye devil, I will. [*Sings.*] " For there's
whiskey in the jar, and there's more behind the bar."

[*Enter* SEPTIMUS SAWYER L. I. E. *Looks at* O'PAFF *in
astonishment.*]

Sawyer. Well upon my word! that fellow seems to be
enjoying my claret and luncheon. Excuse me sir, but—

O'Paff. Don't mention it sir, join me in a glass of claret.

Sawyer. [*Taking seat.*] You seem to be at home here sir?

O'Paff. I am sir, I have a delightful second story front,
with a veiw of the face of nature

Sawyer. Indeed! I hope the wine is satisfactory sir?

O'Paff. Only medium sir. You can't expect much in
these places.

Sawyer. Really! Well sir, allow me to inform you that
I imported that wine myself, for my own private consumption.

O'Paff. I beg your pardon sir, I had no idea that I was trespassing upon private property.

Sawyer. [*Mollified.*] Oh don't mention it. You're quite welcome, permit me to do the honors. [*Sawyer fills glass.*] Mr.—Mr—?

O'Paff. O'Paff sir, Felix O'Paff, Attorney at Law, New York, late of Dublin Four Courts, at your service.

Sawyer. [*Surprised.*] Not the O'Paff who last month conducted the defense in the case of the " Commonwealth *vs.* Forsdyke "?

O'Paff. The same sir.

Sawyer. I'm glad to know you sir. [*Shaking hands.*] Your alibi was one of the completest and best worked up I have ever known.

O'Paff. Thank you for the compliment. And you are one of us yourself then, I take it.

Sawyer. Yes we are two of a kind. My name is Sawyer, Septimus Sawyer.

O'Paff. [*Shaking his hand.*] Delighted to know one so honored and eminent in his profession.

Sawyer. I should judge you were enjoying a large and remunerative practice, Mr. O'Paff.

O'Paff. There's no question as to the enjoyment. In regard to the " large and remunerative," silence is golden.

Sawyer. Indeed ; you surprise me.

O'Paff. I'm glad to know it sir. It confirms the wisdom of my policy. I always make it a rule to keep up appearances. Let me fill your glass, sir. I have learned that if a man is poor, and acts poor, the very dogs in the street will bark at him.

Sawyer. You're something of a philosopher, O'Paff.

O'Paff. I'm an Irishman, the terms are synonomous.

Sawyer. You always appeared to be overrun with business.

O'Paff. A part of my policy, sir, and all a sham.

Sawyer. Sham ?

O'Paff. Bogus, allow me—[*Fills glass.*] Over this glass of rosy wine I'll let you into the secret of my business activity. My sole capital at present is a smart office boy and a big green bag. The boy is stuffed full of deviltry, and the green bag is stuffed full of old newspapers. I have a desk and several chairs, but they are only hired. And so by dint of keeping up appearances, and seeming not to want it, I'm picking up a stray brief now and then.

Sawyer. There's no fear of your ultimate success, But the problem of living in the interim?

O'Paff. I'm in receipt of a small allowance from an old uncle's estate. I receive it quarterly. The first two weeks I live in clover. It's during the other eleven that the problem comes in, just at present I'm in the eighth week. A lack of confidence seemed to pervade the boarding houses on my circuit, so I slipped over to the island here in search of a retreat, where my personal charms and conversational brilliancy would be an equivalent for my board until next quarter-day. [*Both laugh heartily.*] By the way Sawyer what sort of quarters are these here?

Sawyer. Oh, so, so.

O'Paff. Good provision for the inner man?

Sawyer. Very fair, the old lady provides well, but the cooking is bad, services bad, she means well but don't know.

O'Paff. I see, good heart and bad liver. [*Both laugh.*] Now with my New York landlady its the reverse.

Sawyer. How's that.

O'Paff. Good liver, but no heart, no heart, that's why I'm changing.

Sawyer. [*Laughing, rising and x's to* c.] Well O'Paff, old boy, you must excuse me, my clerk is waiting for me inside with some briefs for me to look over.

O'Paff. Certainly, don't neglect business.

Sawyer. I intended leaving this stupid place to-day, but now that a congenial spirit has been found, I'll stay another week.

O'Paff. Stay a fortnight.

Sawyer. I'll stay a month.

O'Paff. D—n it we'll stay all summer. [*Both laugh,* SAWYER *exits into house roaring.*] It was my lucky star that brought me here, Sawyer is a brick as well as a successful lawyer and I'll cultivate him.

SIR RANDALL BURNS *enters at back coming down* C. *and going toward house.*

I ought to know that face. I beg your pardon sir— [*Sir Randall turns.*] I can't be mistaken, Sir Randall Burns.

Sir Randall. [*Surprised.*] What! Why yes it is. [*Grasps* O'PAFF's *hand.*] Felix O'Paff! My old Trinity College chum!

• *O'Paff.* The same, well this is a pleasant surprise.

Sir Randall. Who could have thought of meeting you here?

O'Paff. Or yourself either. The last time we met, was at the Army and Navy Club rooms in London. It was let me see—

Sir Randall. Three years ago, old fellow.

O'Paff. Exactly. I remember now, just at that time I was a little—

Sir Randall. [*Laughing*] A little hard pushed financially, I remember.

O'Paff. Exactly.

Sir Randall. And now?

O'Paff. I've been holding my own bravely ever since.

Sir Randall. But your uncle left you a handsome property?

O'Paff. In trust, with a quarterly allowance. But the time limit expires in six months from this very day, when I shall receive a snug little fortune.

Sir Randall. In the meantime you know where you can always find a banker.

O'Paff. Meaning yourself, thank you old boy, but I value your friendship too highly, to make myself your debtor.

Sir Randall. Still the same old O'Paff.

O'Paff. I hope so. A little older and a trifle wiser but unchanged in my first principles. But tell me of yourself.

Sir Randall. Well you know I bought a commission and went into the army.

O'Paff. I joined the bar, and went into bankruptcy.

Sir Randall. I served a year, and at Rourke's Drift won the Victoria Cross.

O'Paff. I practiced three years at the Four Courts and never took a brief.

Sir Randall. I sold out my commission and made a tour of the watering places in France and England

O'Paff. I was sold out by a sheriff, made a *de*tour to avoid my creditors, and came to America to retrieve my fortunes.

Sir Randall. At Bath, I met my fate in the lovely Helen Montague.

O'Paff. Poor devil and she jilted you?

Sir Randall Confound it man, no.

O'Paff. What! You're married? Worse and worse. •

Sir Randall. No! Hang it! Don't interrupt me, where did I leave off?

O'Paff. Well I don't know where you left off. You began with Helen Montague.

Sir Randall. I fell desperately in love with her, and at the very moment when I fancied I had some hope of a return of my affection, she disappeared, leaving no clue behind her. Judge of my joyful surprise when a month ago, by the merest accident, I encountered her here in New York where she has relatives.

O'Paff. Sir Randall personally and professionally, I condole with you. There's my card, and if yourself or the lady contemplate an action for abandonment or breach of promise, I'll serve you for friendship's sake.

Sir Randall [*Laughing.*] Thanks you rascal, but I'm not likely to need you in *that* direction, though possibly I may in another, I am confident that Mrs. Montague, who is a widow, has some serious family troubles. I know that I am not indifferent to her, yet some secret in her life keeps me at bay upon the subject of marriage. I'll introduce you, and knowing you to be both a lawyer and a friend she may eventually confide in you.

O'Paff. Leave it to me, my great specialty is widows, and family mysteries is my strong point.

MRS. MONTAGUE *appears on Veranda* R.

Mrs. Montague. Back again. Sir Randall?

Sir Randall. Yes, I just ran down to the village for my mail.

MRS. MONTAGUE, *comes down* R.C.

Allow me to present a friend Mrs. Montague, an old Dublin College chum, Felix O'Paff.

Both acknowledge introduction.

[*Aside to* MRS. MONTAGUE.] An eccentric fellow but generous to a fault. Well born and a gentleman.

Mrs. Montague. I shall like him for your sake.

Sir Randall. Thank you.

O'Paff. Surely it was something more than accident that brought me here to-day.

Organ heard off L.U. E.. *and Ritta singing, at end of strain.*

Mrs. Montague. Music. Are we to have a concert?

[O'PAFF *has gone up* C. *looking off.*

Sir Randall. So it seems, by some exiles from Italia with barrel organ accompaniment.

O'Paff. I declare its my little protege. [*Coming down.*] Here's an interesting case, the face of a madonna and the voice of a nightingale and a form as dainty as a poet's fancy. She's the companion of a villanous old organ grinder who ill-treats her.   About a month ago I caused the rascal's arrest and prosecuted him myself, I could have given him six months on the island, but I let him off on promise of good conduct.   But I've kept him under my eye constantly, for I have felt instinctively that the girl was not his child.

Mrs. Montague. Possibly some waif, that he has picked up ?

O'Paff. Or *stolen*, when she was too young to remember it. [*Organ plays, and* RITTA *sings, coming on with last bars of the music, and leaning over the fence, holding out tambourine for largess* GIOVANNI CONTI *follows her, and both are surrounded by a group of village gamins.   Guests appear on balcony and veranda of hotel.*]

Ritta. [*Holding out tambourine.*] Please Signors, please pretty Signorita remember la pouvra Italiano.

O'Paff. Certainly my darling.

O'PAFF *takes her tambourine and passes it around, and returns it to her.* CONTI *seizes the money.* RITTA *seems delighted and surprised to see* O'PAFF, CONTI *sullen and angry.*

Was I right, Mrs. Montague ?

Mrs. Montague. You were indeed, Mr O' Paff.   The girl is as sweet and dainty as a violet.   Do you think she would sing for us ?

O'Paff. To be sure, that's what she's here for.   I'll warrant she'll not be troubled with the chronic cold that affects your professional vocalist upon all social occasions. [*Goes up to gate* C.] Come in dear. [RITTA *hesitates frightened and looks to* CONTI *for authority.*] Come child you're among friends here, have no fear.

[*Urges her in and down* C.   CONTI *follows with organ, children bringing up rear.*]

The lady would like to hear you sing, dear.

Mrs. Montague. Yes, please oblige us.

Ritta. I don't a know.   [*Looks to Conti.*

Conti. Si, sing a de song for a de lady.

RITTA *sings, accompanied by* CONTI *with the organ.   All applaud.* RITTA *passes tambourine.   Ladies on balcony drop coins down to her.   She curtsies to all.*

SONG.

LA POUVRA ITALIANO.

Air: La Donna Mobile—*Rigolletto.*

Ritta. Far over land and sea
Lies my sweet country,
Where songs of melody,
 Ever are thrilling,
'Tho' bright skies ever shine,
And flowers and vine entwine,
Poverty there was mine,
 Each young life killing.
*L'*America's welcome shore,
*L'*America's plenty store,
 Gives to the needy Italiano.
Pouvra, Pouvra, Italiano,
 Pouvra Italiano.

Ritta. [*As she takes money from each.*] I tank a you, I tank a you, vi ringrazio. [CONTI *follows her with his eyes savagely, and when she approaches him siezes the money stealthily.*]

Mrs. Montague. She has an exquisite voice. My child— she really is but a child, who taught you?

Ritta. Taught a me?

Mrs. Montague. Yes who taught you to sing?

Ritta. I don't a know. Who teach a de bird how to sing in de tree? Who teach a de sun to shine? de rain to fall? De same a one teach a me. He teacha evera' one to sing in Italia. So fader Conti say.

O'Paff. There's an answer full of native eloquence.

Mrs. Montague. In what part of Italy were you born?

Ritta. I don't rememb'.

Conti. [*Savagely, half aside*] Bugiardo! Stupido. [*Fawning and smiling.*] Ritta Neapolitan.

O'Paff. Let the girl answer for herself. Were you born in Italy, dear.

[RITTA *frightened looks at* CONTI. *He frowning savagely.*]

Ritta. I don't a rememb'.

O'Paff. You have no remembrance of Italy.

Ritta. [*Frightened.*] No.

Conti. [*Savagely, aside to* RITTA] Piccolo bugiardo. [*You little liar.*] Vieni Sciocco. [*Come away you fool.*] [*Cringing and smiling.*] Buona Sera Signori, come a Ritta.

KITTY *enters from house wildly ringing a large dinner bell,
and shouting " dinner, dinner," she makes a circuit of the
stage, ringing the bell and shouting and enters house still
ringing. Guests all enter house.*

Mrs. Montague. Good bye, Ritta. [*Gives her hand.*] You
must come and sing for us often.

Sir Randall. Here child. [*Gives her large coin.*] Good
bye, petite, come O'Paff.

[*Gives his arm to Mrs. Montague, they enter house.*

O'Paff. I'm with you. Remain here child and I'll send
you out a bit of luncheon. [*Speaks to her aside, Conti watching savagely.*] Here's my address child, if this man ill-treats
you, report to me promptly. You are not afraid to trust me?

Ritta. Oh no, you are a de first a one to speak a kind to
me. It a mak'a me a love you so. Vi ringrazio.

[*Shaking his hand, kissing it and concealing card in her breast.*

O'Paff. Wiping away a tear, a half comic cry.] D——n
it what's the matter with me? [*Hurries into house.*

Conti. [*Siezes Ritta roughly.*] Piccolo bugiardo. What
a for a you say you never a was in Italia?

Ritta. Me not a say a so, Conti.

Conti. Mentitore. [*You lie.*] What a for a you speak a
de Americano? you some a time meet a him.

Ritta. No. Conti. I never a see a heem one time, only
wid a you.

Conti. You lie, beasta. Give a me a de mon. [*Snatches
coin given her by Sir Randall, and rudely pushes her.*] You
try a deceive a me, I kill a you. You some a time see a de
Americano alone. Voi pentirede. [*You shall repent.*]

Ritta. It isn't a true Conti. I swear a it by a de memory
of a my a mother.

Conti. Den what a make a heem give a you a de let?
Mee a see. Give a me de let.

Ritta. You're a mistake. Dio! abbia pieta di zuesta orfana.
[*God have pity on the orphan.*]

Conti. Miserabile impostare. What for a you a say you
not rememb' Italia. I always tell a you what a say. You
try a make a dem a tink you not my child. Confess a to a .
me de trut?

Ritta. I have a noting to confess.

Conti. You lie, beasta. [*Seizing her roughly.*] Give a
me a de let, or I a kill a you. [*Savagely.*]

O'PAFF *appears in door of house* R. CONTI *passes* RITTA, *over to* L., *leaving himself between* O'PAFF *and* RITTA.

O'Paff. Stop! you black muzzled villian. Don't dare to lay the weight of a finger upon that child. You've had one taste of the law. The next time you'll not get off so easy.

Conti. [*Cringing and smiling.*] Oh, you're a mistake, I not a beat a my child. I love a my a child more a dan I love a my a self. But some a time she not a mind a me, I a scold a her a little, no a more. De fader must a make a de child mind.

O'Paff. Tell me, child, has this man been beating you?

[RITTA *wants to speak but fears to do so.*

Conti. Me a beat a my a child! Oh, Signor! Ritta did I a beat a you? [*Fawning.*]

O'Paff. Silence you blackguard, and let the child speak for herself. Look up, child, you are in a land now where the law will protect you, even against your own father. Has he been abusing you again?

[RITTA *wants to speak, but* CONTI *is glaring at her savagely.*]

Ritta. [*Sullenly.*] No.

Conti. You see a Signor, you was a mistake. Come a Ritta, we must a go a home.

[*They pass up* C., RITTA *looking longingly at* O'PAFF, *he presses her hand assuringly.*]

O'Paff. You know where to find me when you want a friend or protector.

[*She kisses his hand,* CONTI *takes her by the hand.*

Conti. Come a Ritta. Buono Sera Signor. Vieni Stupido. [*Come away, fool.*] Io lo detesto. [*I hate him.*]

[*They exit through gate and off,* RITTA *looking back longingly,* CONTI *savagely.*]

O'Paff. I'm not quite sure that I'm doing right in letting the girl continue with the old scoundrel. But I'll keep a close eye on him from this time forward. I don't know what the devil has made me take such an interest in that child.

Enter HOFFMEIER *at back, looks after* CONTI *as he comes down.*

O'Paff. Hello! Hoffmeier, what brings you over here?

Hoffmeier. Oh, several tings, but principally I'm piping off your old friend, Conti, dere.

O'Paff. What have you learned about him since I saw you?

Hoffmeier. Vell I haf learned dot he lives in a den in Crosby street, and have learned enough to make me dink de place is a fence.

O'Paff. A what?

Hoffmeier. A fence; receiver of stolen goods.

O'Paff. Oh, I see

Hoffmeier. Und dis organ grinding bisness is only a blind for somding else.

O'Paff. But what did you learn about his record here?

Hoffmeier. He came here three years ago von London.

O'Paff. Did the girl come with him?

Hoffmeier. Yah, und registered at Castle Garden as his child.

O'Paff. But there was no mother registered at the time?

Hoffmeier. No.   There's an old crone called Mother Rosa, who keeps the den in Crosby street for him while he vas away, bud she has only been there aboud six months.   The place is a kind of a resort for suspicious characters, such as sneak thieves.

O'Paff. I think we have capital enough to start on.

Hoffmeier. I'm going to make a round of some of dem Crosby and Baxter street dens dis evening.   Vould you like to go along?

O'Paff. I would, as a student.

Hoffmeier. Der may be some cutting und slashing.

O'Paff. All the more interesting.   I'm with you.

Hoffmeier. Vell you can leave here mit de sefen o'clock boad, und I vill meet you by de Metropolitan Hodel.

O'Paff. All right, Hoffmeier. I'll be there at nine o'clock, sharp.   Excuse me old boy, but I left my friends at dinner.
                                        [*Exit* O'PAFF *into house.*

Hoffmeier. Oh, dots all right.   I thought dis place vould suid O'Paff, ven I dold him aboud it.   I'll yust slip down around de vater pond, und see if I can get my eye on dot English tief.   [*Music. Exit* HOFFMEIER, L. I. E.

Enter JIMMIE NIPPER *at back, sneaking, peering about cautiously.*

Jim. H'all h'of the swells h'is h'at dinner now h'i guess. [*Looks in at door, then looks in through gauze window facing audience, then goes up at back of house.*] I 'opes as 'ow there ar'nt no dogs 'ere, for I 'ates dogs, I does.   Dogs 'an me 'as a naterel h'antipathy.   [*Looking off* R.]   Vy there's a vindow 'open, h'it must go h'in to a bed-room.   [*Looks about.*]   Not a blooming soul in sight, so 'ere goes.

[*Exit off behind house* R., *music stops.*

Enter SAWYER *from house, tipsy, napkin under chin, etc., etc.*

Sawyer.   O'Paff's a brick, hic, very glad I didn't leave to-day as I intended, hic, it's astonishing how that lobster salad affects me, hic, always did, hic.   I could'nt stand it in there any longer, hic.   What with that jolly Irishman's reminiscences, and the beautiful widow's champagne, hic, —no I mean the widow's beautiful cham, hic, pagne,— no, I was right before, hic—the beautiful widow's cham, hic, she *is* a beauty.   Dear me, hic, it *is* astonishing about that hic, salad, must have been some new kind of oil in it, hic, it, I'm very weary, hic.   [*Drops into rustic seat under window of house.*]   I like that Irishman, hic, when my old partner Flint retires next year, hic, damme if I don't take O'Paff in as a full partner.   The firm needs some young blood. [*Dozing off.*]   Irish blood, hic, [*Yawns.*]   I think I'll take a quiet forty winks.

Curls up on bench.   Music hurry, low at first to swell forte with action to end act.   Screams heard in house, cries of " thief," " robbers," " murder," ' burglars," etc., etc. Guests rush out as if from dinner, with napkins, etc., etc.   A terrific glass crash, then working crash, and JIMMY NIPPER *flies through the gauze window, falling over* SAWYER *on the bench.   A large bull-dog is hanging to the seat of Jim's pantaloons, his coat is ripped up the back, a fright wig on, Jim is yelling, the dog flying in the air behind him as he runs.*   SAWYER *gathers himself up.*   MRS. TARBOX *and* KITTY *get to* C. *of stage* MRS. TARBOX R *and* KITTY L. C., SIR RANDALL *and* HELEN *on veranda, other guests filling the stage.*   MR. CRANE *rushes out to* L. COR.   O'PAFF, *napkin under chin rushes to* C. *just as* NIPPER *rushes out.   The dog hanging to* JIM *knocks* KITTY *and* MRS. TARBOX *so that they fall into* O'PAFF'S *arms, one on each side.   Ring*

ON THIS SITUATION.

ENCORE.

SAWYER, R., CRANE, L., *both laughing at* O'PAFF *with the two women.*   O'PAFF *gives them both a bounce, throwing* MRS. TARBOX *into* SAWYER'S *arms, and* KITTY *into* CRANE'S.   *Music hurry continues.*   O'PAFF *starts up* C. JIM *with dog hanging to him rushes on* L. I. E., *yelling, followed by* HOFFMEIER.   *They rush up and off* C., *the dog hitting* O'PAFF, *he drops into seat* R. C., *back.   A "dude" fellow and a lady are coming down* C. *just in time to meet* JIM, *the lady is knocked into* O'PAFF'S *lap, and the "dude" falls across hammock.   Screaming and general confusion, kept up until curtain falls on last picture.*   SAWYER *struggling to hold up* MRS. TARBOX, CRANE *same with* KITTY, *both kicking and screaming Music forte.*

CURTAIN.

ACT II.

SCENE.—*The cellar of Giovanni Conti in Crosby Street, New York. A stone cellar, entrance door in upper part of flat* L., *landing in front of door, stairway leading from landing to* C. *of stage, with turn so that last two steps face audience, strong railing on landing and staircase, upper door must open down stage towards* L., *door under landing.* [*practical.*] *Set fireplace* R. 3 E., *with mantel, on which is statuette of Virgin, above mantel, a small panel* [*painted in to match scene,*] *hinged to open down, resting on mantel, to open during business of scene,* [*supposed to be receptacle for stolen goods*]. *In upper part of* R. *flat, small semi-circular grated window painted in, lower part of flat an alcove or vault painted as if running under sidewalk, with old barrels, junk,* &c. *Fire burning in fire-place, table* R., *stool and common chair, small bar at back with glasses, bottles,* &c., *pitcher on bar, rough benches around stage, stool* L., *lots of rags on stage* R. [*Rosa discovered.*]

Rosa. [*An old Italian crone assorting rags,* R.] La Bella Signoritta, quando si returno? All de day in de street, all de night in de dark room to sleep. Poor Ritta! she too pretty, too good for dis place, too good a fore dese people. She come a to no good here. Conti villano? no keep a promise wid Rosa, bring a me here to watch Ritta when he go away. Promise me a every ting, give a me noting, and treat a me like a slave. Ah Sacrista! I have a one time a little child myself, she die and leave a poor old Rosa alone, long a time ago. But some a time when I look at Ritta, I seem a too see de face of my own innocent child, dead! dead! dead! Ah Sacrista! me a so tired, so tired. [*She starts as* COCKNEY JIM *appears upon platform* L. *flat.*] Who come a dare? [*Recognizes* JIM.] Ah! is dat a you, Jim?

Jim. [*Coming down steps.*] Vy incorse it is, who did you think it vas, the Lord Mayor? Bon sour, old mother Rosa, vitch means h'I'm glad to get home. [*Throughout scene* JIM *quietly conveys the idea that he is rather sore from the effect of the bull-dog incident at end of previous act, using great care to avoid vulgarity*] Vere's old Conti and the pretty kid?

Rosa. Not a come a home yet.

Jim. Vat, not got back from 'is tower hinto the country for 'is 'ealth, vell, 'e h'is a goin' of it.

Rosa. Take a chair, Jim, sit a down, resta.

Jim Vot?

Rosa. Take a de chair.

Jim. [*Makes motion as though to sit down, then stops suddenly*] No thank you, old voman, hi prefers to stand, hi can digest my wittals better. Hi say, is there anyone 'ere [*Mysteriously.*]

Rosa. No, me alone all de day, all de night. [*Eagerly.*] You have a someting to sell?

Jim. Vy incorse I'av. Vot do you suppose I was a doin' of all this time, travelling for my 'ealth?

Rosa. Nobody will a come, [*eagerly.*] quick a Jim, what have a you got?

Jim. Now don't get havoricious old voman, vait. [*Goes to sit, jumps up, then very carefully sits on back of chair, his feet on the seat.*] Now then, old voman, what do you say to that pair o' shoes? As I vas a passin' a shoe store, a daug flew at my calf, hi set another daug to fight with 'im and vile the boy vas a partin' of 'em, I borrowed these for my trouble. 'Ere's a seal-skin cap made of wool as was growed on the back of the royal helephant of Siam.

Rosa. [*Eagerly.*] You have a someting more?

Jim. Vy incoorse, 'ere's a nobby locket and chain as I borrowed from a blessed baby as was playin' on a stoop with it, poor little think, it broke my 'eart to do it, and it a lookin' at me so hinnocent like, but hi know if hi didn't take it, some bloomin' willian would come along and steal it, and the blessed hinfant would get walloped for losin' it. 'Ere ve are again, as they say at the show, ha dozen solid silver spoons, as vos presented to me by a lady on Staten Hisland. She vas agoin' to give me the rest of the set, but I 'adn't time to vait.

Rosa. You have a something more?

Jim. 'Av I? h'aint I? I've been busy to day. [*Pulls silk handkerchiefs from his neck, sleeves, pants-legs, &c., about ten or a dozen in all.*] Silk vipes as was made from lambs as vos exported from H'Africa, Ten dollars for the lot.

Rosa. Oh, no! no! no! No good a silk, very bad, tree doll for all, dare. [*Gives coin.*]

Jim. Vot, three dollars! Vell this is the most ungrate-fulest vorld I vos ever in. Vy the shoes is vorth more alone. The man as made em lived with 'is mother, and didn't pay no board, or hi couldn't sell em for quarter hof the money.

Rosa. A you rob a poor old Rosa, dere tak a de tree doll.

Jim. Vell, 'ere's honreasonableness. Takin' adwantage of a poor little horfan as haint got no father nor no mother. There aint no encouragement for business henterprise. It almost tempts me to turn honest. Well, shell out.

Rosa. Good boy, Jim. Bona! Bona! you shall have a some a wine wid a Rosa.

Jim. Hexcuse me. Hi haint ready to commit susanside yet, ven I ham, hi'll drink some of your wine. Give me the pitcher old voman, and hi'll get some beer; beer's 'olesome, vine aint, leastwise not your brand [*She hands him stone-pitcher.*]

Rosa. [*Chuckling.*] Aha! Jim too much a particular.

Jim. [*Going up steps.*] Praps I his, praps I hisn't. But hi hobjects to bein' pizened vith either wittals or my drinkin'.
[*Exit* JIM *off door* 1. *flat.*

MUSIC.—ROSA *looks hurriedly around, then goes to mantel-piece* R. 3 E., *removes images, crucifix, &c. from mantel, touches spring, and stone over mantel falls down or re-volves, showing a receptacle into which she places the stolen articles; then replaces images, &c. on mantel as before, after touching spring and returning panel to its place.*

Rosa. [*Gloating.*] Aha! no policeman can find him dere. Aha! Rosa no fool; all a safe a now; all a safe a now.

MUSIC.—*Enter onto platform* RITTA *followed by* CONTI *with his organ, he pushes her before him into room, and down the stairs, following her savagely.* RITTA *down* L. C., CONTI *places organ at back.*

Conti. [*Savagely.*] So you wont a come home, hey? Bestia! You don't a rememb' Italy, hey? You shall re-pent.

Ritta. I have a noting to repent. What for you treat a me so to-day? I do no wrong. I tell a no story. I give a you all de mon.

Conti. You lie, beasta! you speak a someting secret wid de Americano, den you refuse a tell a me, den you talk of run away.

Ritta. I work a for you all de day in de street, and get hungry and tirsty, and never complain one time, den you beat a me and bring a me to dis miserable den, to sleep on de floor among a de rags and eat like a de dog in de street. You cannot be my father, or you would love a me, and not treat a me so.

Conti. [*Savagely.*] Sacra Madonna! [*Threatening her.*] Lasciate questa camera! [*Leave the room.*] Do me not carry de org all de day? You have a only to sing a de song, and get a de compliment from a de lady and de gentleman. I treat a you too kind, don't me buy you de fine clothes to wear, and me wear de old a won? via.

Ritta. And why do you buy me de fine dress? Dat I may please de eye of de Signori, dat I may listen to dere insults, and den bring you de price. O, my Mother, whose love I have never known, look a down in pity on your a poor child, whose heart is so sick to-night.

Conti. Go to your room for de present. Dis night before you sleep, I will have understand wid you.

[CONTI *sits angrily at table* R. C.

Ritta. [*Aside.*] Miserabile Impostare! I am a determine. Voglio essere libero. [*I will be free.*] [*Looking at O'Paff's card.*] I have de card of de brave Signore, when Jim comes home he shall take it for me; Jim has good a heart, he will a befriend a me. I never come a back again.

[*Exit door under stairway* L.

Conti. [*At table, aside.*] Avro vendetta. Ritta getting too old for me to trust alone, some a day she leave a me, den my plot and plan I lay so well for all a dese a year, come to noting, and now just when *he* has a come back, and I can begin a to play my card for de great property, *she*, who is to bring a me all, begin to rebel, and talk of leave me. Sacramento! She must go on de street no more, dis night I conquer her.

Rosa. [*Placing wine and glass on table.*] Giovanni you come a home late to night. What was a de mat wid Ritta?

Conti. She talk about a leave a me, about a run away. Aha, bestia! I kill her when she try to run away.

Rosa. [*Aside.*] Poor Ritta.

Conti. [*Aside.*] She shall not a leave me now, just when de time has come dat she can make a me *rich*, rich, rich, like a de lord.

Rosa. [*Eagerly.*] Ritta can make Conti rich; how?

Conti. [*Savagely, pushing her away.*] Not a your a business. Vui de gui. [*Stand aside.*] Stupido.

Rosa. [*Aside.*] Sacrista! He treat me like a de dog. Io lo detesto. [*I hate him.*] Some a day he be sorry villano.

COCKNEY JIM *enters singing*, CONTI *starts.*

Conti. [*Starting.*] Who's a dare?

Rosa. Only Jim, he bring a some a beer.

JIM *comes down steps with beer, singing "A Pitcher of Beer," puts it on table with last note of song.*

Jim. [*Slapping Conti on back.*] Vot, my rummy old pal, back from your provincial tower, lots of luck, I 'ope?

Conti. [*Sullenly.*] No, not a much, bad a business.

Jim. Just the same vith me.

Conti. Take a de chair, sit a down.

Jim. Vot?

Conti. Take a de seat.

Jim. No, thank you, hi prefers to stand hup and grow. Old voman give hus some crystals. [ROSA *brings down tumblers and places them on table.* JIM *fills one which* ROSA *quickly takes and drinks.*] Twig the old lady, aint she hartful. [*Fills other glass for* CONTI, *being none for himself, takes the pitcher.*] Ere's success to honest henterprise, hall the vorld hover, says I. [*Drinks from pitcher*, CONTI *from glass.*

Conti. Jim, I see to-day, an old friend of yours, who you tink a?

Jim. A hold friend of mine, not the Prince of Vales, I 'opes, for hif Albert should come to New York without a sendin' me 'is card, hi should feel 'urt.

Conti. No, not from London, but from Australia, from Swan a River.   [ROSA *at back listening eagerly.*

Jim. Vot, from Haustralia? *Aside to* CONTI.] Hi say old man, before ve get onto Swan River and Haustralia, don't you think the hold woman 'ad better retire?

Conti. Si Rosa! Leave a de room. Go keep a Ritta company. Lasciate questo luogo. [*Leave the place:*] Via! beasta!

Rosa. [x *to* L., *aside.*] Cosa sara l'intenzione. [*What are they up to.*] He mean a some mischief to Ritta, he shall not harm her, he shall kill old Rosa first. Villano! Io lo

detesto ! [*I hate him.*] Rosa will a watch.   Pouvra Ritta !
you have a *one* friend, old a Rosa, old a Rosa.

[*Exit* ROSA *in door under stairway* L.

Conti. [*Aside.*] Old a hag !   I believe a she would a
betray me too, if she knew the truth.

JIM X's *to bow* ROSA *off at end of her speech,* X's *to* R. *of table.
Bus. of sitting down and jumping up quickly with* "*oh* !"

Conti. What for a you jump ?

Jim. Nothink. [*Aside.*] Oh, but I 'ates daugs. [*Fixes
himself on extreme corner of chair.*] Now then, Conti, fire
away, who vas it?

Conti. Do you remember the great London crook, Jasper
Craddock ?

Jim. Vot ?   Do I remember " Gentleman Jasper "?   Vell
don't hi ?   Many's the crib I've helped 'im to crack.   Vy
vots he a doin' 'ere ?   He had five years to serve ven I left.

Conti. He escape tree years before his time.

Jim. Vell I'm blowed !   'Ere's a go !   Vere is he ?

Conti. Oh, he live a in a great style, Hotel Brunswick.

Jim. Vell that's just like the Captain.   He always vas an
airy cove, but he vos a hartist in his business, and halways
square vith his pals.

Conti. He come a here to-night to see a you.

Jim Coming to see me ?   Vell 'ere's a condescension, hi
suppose hi shall 'ave to dine with 'im to-morrow hat the
Brunswick.   Hi say, Conti, if I vos you, I vould keep Ritta
out of 'is sight, the Captain was always nutty on pretty gals.

Conti. [*Quickly.*] He never see her, he never shall,
[*Aside*] until a de proper time, [*Aloud.*] and don't a you
dare a to mention her name in his presence.   [*Slaps table
savagely.*   JIM, *who has the pitcher to his mouth drinking,
jumps, spitting out beer, then drops back into chair and
jumps up quickly again.*

Jim. 'Ere! Vots the use of frightening a feller that vay ?
I shant say a vord, of course I shant. [*Aside.*] And I'll take
precious good care that she gets hout hov the reach of both
hof 'em afore many days, even if I have to blow on the old
fence and turn honest.

During foregoing scene, ROSA *has shown her face at door
about twice, listening.*

Conti. Hush! Some a one come. [*Enter* JASPER CRAD-
DOCK.] It is a de Captain. [CRADDOCK *has on a disguise
beard, large common over-coat, closely buttoned, soft hat pulled
down over face.*]

Jasper. [*In an assumed voice and manner.*] My good
fellow would you oblige me with a light? Why, what a
curious place. [*Significantly.*] Is it empty?

Conti. Si, empty as a de egg-shell, no policeman near.

Jasper. [*Coming down* C.] Good, glad to hear it, but your
friend?

Jim. [x'g *to him* C.] Vy Capting, this *his* a hunexpected
pleasure. [*They shake hands.*]

Jasper. What, Jim! my young pal, it is you, and Conti
was not lying to me. [*He removes his beard and throws
open his coat, revealing an elegant toilet beneath, clothes in
latest fashion, rather loud display of jewelry, diamonds, &c.*]

Jim. Capting, if I'd a knowed as you was a comin', I
would 'av 'ad my wally de chamber meet you hat the dock
vith my family carriage. Come, Capting, 'ave some beer.

Jasper. The smell of the place is bad enough, without
adding the fumes of stale beer. I say, Conti, why don't you
keep the place clean, bad smells and dirt are not necessary
to safety.

Conti. [x'g *to* L. *taking seat.*] De place is all a right, good
enough for me, good enough for my company.

Jasper. Good enough for you, no doubt, but I haven't
been used to it.

Jim. Vell, aint you a going of it. Hi say, Capting, ve
didn't 'ave such bloomin' fine quarters in Swan River, and
vouldn't ve have given our heyes for a glass of beer or
Shandy Gaff, there. .

Jasper. Stow that, Jim. It consumed twelve of the best
years of my life, and I never want to hear the accursed place
mentioned again.

Jim. Hall right, Capting, hi don't mean to 'arrow hup
hunpleasant memories.

Jasper. Jim, I want five minutes talk with Conti, here, just
stand outside and give us the tip for safety, that's a good
fellow.

Jim [*Going up steps.*] Hall serene, I'll pipe hoff the cops
vile you chin old maccaroni, but don't keep me long,
because my family physician says as 'ow I musn't stand in
the draft.

Exit JIM *door up* L., CRADDOCK *sits on table* R., CONTI *seated on stool* L.

Jasper. Well, Mr. Conti.

Conti. Well, Mr. Craddock.

Jasper. We meet again.

Conti. Noting very strange in dat. People a meet a ever a day. Me never a trouble you

Jasper. Possibly not, but my own mind troubles me.

Conti. What I got a to do wid your a mind.

Jasper. Everything. It is in your power to relieve it.

Conti. Well, what you want a wid me?

Jasper I want an assurance that you have kept faith with me.

Conti. Don't I always keep a fait wid my friend?

Jasper. Oh, see here, Conti, what's the use beating about the bush? You know what I want to get at.

Conti. May be so, may be not.

Jasper. Well then, to make sure, I'll freshen your memory. Twelve years ago in London, a rich old man disinherited his heir, settling a great fortune on his grand-child, in trust to her invalid mother. The old man died, a month later, the child one evening strayed from its nurse, and all search for her proved vain. The invalid mother survived the loss of her child but a few weeks, and then malicious tongues whispered abroad that the disinherited brother had caused the abduction or death of the child, realizing that with father, sister, and niece removed, the property must revert to him. Are these incidents familiar to you?

Conti. It seem a to me, I here some a ting like it.

Jasper. Oh, indeed. But no evidence could be brought to bear to connect him with the abduction. He was about to lay claim to his father's estates, when his name unfortunately got mixed up with others in a large diamond robbery, and with but scant time for preparation he started upon a fifteen years visit to Australia.

Conti. Si, he travel for de benefit of his constitution.

Jasper. Exactly. He left his place of recreation some three years earlier than was expected of him, and came to New York, where he found an old companion, and said to him : " Paulo Viotti, I am about to invoke the law to secure my father's estates in England. Twelve years ago I gave you one hundred pounds to effectually remove an obstacle from my path. Before I could receive your assurance that your work was done, the arm of the law separated us. I now seek the assurance that you have kept faith with me, that there is no LIVING *obstacle* between me and my hopes.

Conti. You tink de Italiano betray his friend, he answer you, *no,* [x'g *to* JASPER.] he do his work a well. Could de bottom of de river Thames speak aloud, it would tell a you dat Viotti keep a his promise to his a friend. [*They shake hands.*]

Jasper. [*Relieved.*] Good! I felt confident that all was clear before me, but I wanted the assurance from your own lips.

Conti. Now you are a satisfy?

Jasper. Yes, now I am satisfied. [*Going* R.]

Conti. [*Aside.*] Some people easy satisfy. [*Going* L.]

Jasper. [*Exultingly.*] To morrow I shall employ counsel to communicate with London agents, and set the train in motion, that is to roll back to me freighted with millions. And once I lay my hands upon my father's estates, with the chink of my gold, I'll silence the tongues that hint at mischief, and with the flash of my diamonds, I'll dazzle the eyes that would scan the pages of the past.

Conti. [*Aside* L.] Oh, he be a great a man! great a man! may be ; what will a Conti be?

Jasper. In the meantime I must live, and as usual, I must live like a gentleman, which means I must do a little of the old business until the tide turns. I have spotted a place that I think will yield something handsome. Are you with me?

Conti. Always ready to make a honest penny.

Jasper. I thought so. [*Whistles a signal.*]

JIM *enters.*

Jim. [*Coming down.*] 'Ere we are Capting.

Jasper. Well, Jim, old pard! Are you game in a little business enterprise?

Jim. Vy, Capting, I shall honly be too proud to renew our business relations.

Jasper. I have a job to-morrow night, a little way out of town.

Jim. And you want me to vork the old vinder racket I suppose?

Jasper. Yes.

Jim. Hi 'opes its night vork, Guv'nor ?

Jasper. Yes, its night work.

Jim. I 'opes they aint got no daugs.

Jasper. Conti, have you got a good set of Safe tools ?

Conti. Si, de best in de market always on hand.

Jasper. Then no more for the present. You two be at the junction of Eighth avenue and Broadway at ten o'clock to-morrow night, and I'll pick you up in my buggy. [*Puts on his beard, buttons coat, &c.*]

Jim. Hi say, Capting give us a couple of car tickets— Buggy riding makes our feet sore.

Jasper. [*Laughs and throws coin on table.*] There. [*Starts up steps, old* ROSA *is seen to peep out of door,* CONTI *sees her and expresses anger in pantomine.*] Now don't forget the tools, and ten sharp.

MUSIC.—CRADDOCK *is about three steps up,* HOFFMEIER *appears in door in full uniform.*

Jasper. [*Assumed manner.*] Oh, might I trouble you for a light, Mr.—Mr.—

Conti. [*Handing him match.*] Conti, my name a Conti. [*returns to seat and commences counting over his pennies.* JIM, *upon Hoffmeier's entrance, pulls out a little pamphlet, and appears absorbed in reading, at table* R.]

Jasper. Oh, officer, making your rounds, eh ? What filthy dens these Italians live in to be sure. I dropped in to light my cigar, but the stench nearly overpowered me. [*They are both now on platform.*] Good evening, Mr.— Mr.—

Hoffmeier. [*Stiffly*] Hoffmeier, Ferdinand Hoffmeier.

Jasper. Oh, yes ; good evening, Mr. Hoffmeier.

[*Exit* CRADDOCK.

Hoffmeier. [*Coming down looking after Craddock.*] That's an odd fish for these waters. I bet he's a crook. Well he's a stranger anyhow. [*Saunters quietly down behind* CONTI.] Ah, good evening, Mr. Conti.

Conti. Buona Sera.

Hoffmeier. Business good to-day ?

Conti. No, Signore, bad a business, bad a business. [*Aside.*] Sacra maladetta. [*Sees* ROSE *listening.*] The old hag ! She play de spy on me, sacrista.

Hoffmeier. [*Saunters quietly about room, approaches door under stairs, which closes, saunters over to mantel* R., *looks at figures on mantel. All very quiet, old* ROSA'S *face is seen watching him as he approaches mantel,* CONTI *also savagely observing him. Drops down to table* R., *at which* JIM *is seated, stands behind table, looks at him.*] Well, young man !

Jim. Go avay, please, can't you see hi'm a studying my Sunday-school verses. [*Dives into his book.*]

Hoffmeier. [*Aside.*] They're a sharp lot. No matter how suddenly I drop in on them, there's never any sign of stolen goods. Good evening, Mr. Conti.

Conti. Buona notte. Beasta !

Jim. Bonie sour. [*Aside.*] 'Ow I 'ates cops.

Hoffmeier. [*At door.*] I wonder where the girl is ? [*Exit.*

Jim. Whew ! 'ow I 'ates folks as comes a snooping around makin, a feller 'old 'is blooming breath for 'alf an 'our. Blest if I musn't 'ave a snooze after that.

Conti. [*Aside, seeing* ROSA'S *face at door.*] Dat old diabolo ! she listen yet, I kill her.

Jim. [*Pulls table up back* R., *and places chair on it for pillow, and climbs onto it.*] Hi say, Conti, Susan forgot to put the shams on my pillows.

MUSIC—ROSA *puts her head through door,* CONTI *is watching,*

Conti. Sacra Madonna ! [*Rushes up and drags* ROSA *out and throws her into* L. *corner.*] [*Savagely.*] What for you listen all de time at de door ? What for you play the spy ?

Rosa. Rosa not a play de spy.

Conti. Bugiardo.

Rosa. No, Rosa not a lie, me only watch for a de property dere, [*points to mantel,*] me no spy Conti.

Conti. Miserable liar ! You betray me !

Rosa. No, no ; me not a betray you. [*She's close to him on this speech.*]

Conti. Bugiardo ! [*Strikes her in the face, she falls* L., *he turns* R., *grabs chair and is in act of rushing upon her when* RITTA *runs between them.*] PICTURE.

Ritta. Stop ! Conti, stand a back. [ROSA *grabs* RITTA'S *hand and kisses it.*]

Rosa. [*Aside savagely.*] He strike a me, like a dog ! Avra Vendetta ! I have a revenge, I have a revenge. [ROSA x's *up back, goes up* R. *to bar.* JIM *is now up looking on.*]

Conti. You play de spy too, you listen at de door ?

Ritta. No, me not a listen.

Conti. How dare you stop a me ?

Ritta. I dare, because only a miserable coward would strike a woman.

Conti. Leave a de room.

Ritta. I will not leave a de room.

Conti. Sacramento! Piccolo villanno! [*Little villian*] You dare to brave a me?

Ritta. Yes, I dare to brave a you.

CONTI, *with an angry gesture, turns, going up* R., *removing his coat as though for a struggle,* ROSA *in action entreats him, he repulses her angrily, still working at coat, she half hanging onto him. This action is kept until he receives cue to strike her.*

Jim. [*Who is part way up stairs, runs down to* RITTA'S *side.*] [*Aside quickly.*] Can I do anything for you, young fellar?

Ritta. Oh yes Jim [*gives O' Paff's card*] tell *him* to come.

Jim. I'd die for you little feller, but don't give me away.

Ritta. No, no! I pray for you.

JIM *runs up steps.* CONTI *hits* ROSA *and knocks her down, then seizes her and drags her over* R *and throws her into room under stairs, closing door. All done very rapidly, turns savagely on* RITTA.

Conti. Now I break a your spirit, or I break a your neck. [JIM *is now just passing out the door*] Jim, lock a de door, and give a me de key.

Jim. Hexcuse me my noble maccaroni chewer, this is a family quarrel, and I don't want to be either a witness or a participitater. [*Exit* JIM, *closing door.*

CONTI, R. C.   RITTA, L. R.

Conti. Now you go into dat room, and stay till I call, via!

Ritta. I will not enter dat miserable den again.

Conti. Den I settle wid you now. I know de Americano give you let, me see you put it in your breast. Give a me.

Ritta. It is not true Conti, I have no let.

Conti. You lie beasta, I make a you tell a me de truth or me kill a you.

Rushes at her, RITTA *draws stiletto and stands on picture.*

Ritta. Stand back Conti. [*pause.*] Me bear a your cruelty no longer.

Conti. Me not cruel, me treat you kind and you try to deceive, to betray me, to have a de secret meeting wid de Americano.

Ritta. You are miserable liar. When I was little child, I work for you all de day, and all de night, and you starve and beat a me, and I bear it all for I know no better. Ritta is woman now, and I be your slave no more. [CONTI *springs at her.*] Stop Conti, or me a strike!

Conti. Sacra maladetta! You would not dare to use de weapon on your own father.

Ritta. You are not my father.

Conti. Who tell you dat?

Ritta. My own heart tell me.

Conti. Den your heart a lie.

Ritta. No the voice of nature cannot lie.

Conti. Your fadder command a you drop a de stiletto.

Ritta. No, you go your a way, I go mine. Do not try to prevent a me. You teach a me de use of dis weapon to defend my honor, try to stop me now, you shall see I learn your lesson well.

CONTI *is down* R. RITTA C *backing up toward steps.*

Conti. [*Changing manner and stealthily gathering up blanket on floor by his side.*] Why Ritta, your fadder would not a hurt a you. [*crawling up on her.*] Me speak only for your good.

He throws blanket over her head and seizes her roughly, gets stiletto and throws her down into R *corner, standing on picture, between* RITTA *and stairway.*

Conti. Now we see which is de stronger, your will or mine. [RITTA *starts up.*] Stand a where you are. First I lock a de door. [CONTI, *starts up steps*

Ritta. Yes lock a de door! The God of de orphan will protect me.

Conti. [*Running up steps.*] We shall see, we shall see.

[*As he reaches the door it is thrown open and* O'PAFF *confronts him.* PICTURE. *Conti shrinking back over stair-railing.* O'PAFF *has his overcoat on his arm.*

Ritta. [*Down* R, *kneeling.*] Heaven has sent an angel to me.

CONTI *backs stealthily down into room followed by* O'PAFF. *As* CONTI *reaches* C. R., RITTA *tries to rush by him, he seizes her by the throat and forces her down at his feet* R., *standing knife in hand between* RITTA *and* O'PAFF O'PAFF *is on the third step.*

Conti. [*Savagely.*] What you want a here?

O' Paff. Speak child, do you want to leave this place?

Ritta. [*Imploringly.*] Oh yes take a me away from dis place, take a me away from dis man.

O' Paff. Mr. Conti, I'll trouble you for that young woman.

Conti. And I trouble you to leave dis place, dis is a my house, dis is my child, dis is her home. You have a no right to trespass. You put your foot on dat floor, and I kill a you like I kill a dog. [*He stands with knife in left hand, holding* RITTA *at his feet, with right hand at her throat, on the words "kill a dog,"* RITTA *bites his hand, he turns quickly with a cry of pain, and* O'PAFF *on the instant throws his overcoat over* CONTI's *head, and jumps onto him like a tiger.*

O' Paff. Quick, Ritta ; run for your life. [RITTA *runs up steps.*] [*Struggling.*] Drop that knife you murderin' villian, or I'll strangle you first and kill you afterwards.

O'PAFF *throws* CONTI *into* R. *corner, and runs up steps,* CONTI *gathers himself quickly and rushes after him.* O'PAFF *is about three steps up when* CONTI *reaches foot of steps.* O'PAFF *deals him a terrible blow full in the face.* CONTI *spins round like a top, and fall at full length* R., *near footlights. At same moment,* HOFFMEIER *appears in door, receiving* RITTA. O'PAFF *slowly ascending stairs.*

CURTAIN.

ENCORE PICTURE.

CONTI *is up and standing* R. *on picture of baffled rage. Hoffmeier half-way down stairs with club upraised.* O'PAFF *passing out door with* RITTA.

ACT III.

SCENE—*One year later. The Boudoir of* HELEN MONTA-
GUE, *Madison Ave., New York.*

Large bow window C., *an opening* R. C., *showing a corridor
leading off to the* R., *a hat-rack in rear of this corridor,
with umbrella-stand and chair beside it. Handsome curtains across this entrance, drawn aside and looped up. An
opening* L., *of a similar character, which leads to dressing
room. The room is seen beyond partially disclosing a
dressing-table and looking-glass, with hooks upon which are
hung ladies dresses, curtains over this entrance also looped
up, a handsome fire-place* R., *with fire-irons, fender, large
soft rug, footstools on each side. A lounge is placed oblique
in front of the fire-place. Table by the side of the head of
the lounge. Large handsome cloth over the table. Books
upon it, a Lady's work basket containing some fancy work,
a cottage piano* L., *across* 3 E., *an opening* L. 2 E., *showing
a corridor, also with a single curtain over the opening,
drawn aside. Handsome screen set up stage* R., *low in
height, intending to keep the head from draughts only.
Handsome carpet down. Soft rugs at each doorway.
Soft lounging chairs scattered around. Music scattered on
top of piano. A bookcase by its side. Flowers and shrubs
at window. Handsome (drop gas) lamp on the table, half
turned down. Clock on* C., *of mantel. Moonlight scene
outside at back.*

*Kitty discovered dozing in an arm chair.—the front bell
at* R.U.E. *rings,—then a pause—then rings violently—she
jumps up.*

Kitty. Sure the fire's in the next street, or them fire bells
would'nt be making such a row and disturbing people.
[*Yawning.*] Oh bother, to wake me out of me pleasant
nap. Sure they won't be home 'till eleven o'clock, and Iv'e
lots of time for a dacent forty winks. [BELL..] [*Settles herself
again for a sleep when the bell rings louder. She is now
thoroughly awake.*] Be jabers there's the door bell, who can
it be? Faith I'm afraid to go to it, and me all alone by
meself in the house. [*Goes over to the fire place.*] Ah! let
'em ring, and just to think that the beautiful widdy should

fancy a poor Irish girl like me and make a French maid
of me. [*Looking at clock.*] Holy Mother o' Moses, it's
after eleven—that must be them, and all the while I thought
it was the fire engines.

MUSIC—*Runs off* R. U. E., *reenters immediately, preceding*
COCKNEY JIM *who is disguised as a seedy clergyman—
black frock coat, high hat, ragged black gloves, goggles.*
Kitty. Phat name did you say, sir?
Jim. Bilkins, miss, Theophilus Bilkins, marm, as is
chairman of the society for the Propagation of the Heathen
in furrin parts.
Kitty. Well the Misses is'nt in.
Jim. Vot? she hisn't.
Kitty. Will you sit down and wait, sir?
Jim. I vill, ven I've viped my feet. [*Rubbing feet on
carpet.*]
Kitty. The mat is in the hall, sir.
Jim. Vell, you need'nt get it for me.
           [JIM *sighs extravagantly as he takes a seat.*
Kitty. Ain't you feeling well, sir?
Jim. Hi suffer. [*Sighs.*] Hit's a sweet think to suffer,
it makes us 'umble.
Kitty. Well, he's a peculiar animal anyhow.
Jim. Might hi trouble you for a glass of water?
Kitty. [*Going* L.] Yes sir—I'll not be long.
Jim. Don't 'urry on my haccount.
Kitty. I don't like that cratur; if he was'nt a preacher I'd
close the door agin him, but he slipped in before I could.
Any way I'll lock up those spring chickens, for I heard Mr.
O'Paff say that preachers was all fond of spring chickens.
[*Exit* L., *during above speech* JIM *has been craning his neck
as though taking in every detail of the room.*
Jim. [*Dropping assumed manner, runs quickly to room*
R., *and takes it in hurriedly.*] ·Just as Conti said—that's the
young lady's room vot wears so many sparks—and no man
in the 'ouse but the 'ostler, and 'e's in the stable. [*Goes to
window* C. *and tries it.*] I 'ates people vot fastens their
vinders. [*Unfastens window, opens it and looks out on balcony.*] Conti was right again—the vindy opens on a side
balcony honly four feet from the ground. Vi hi could
strangle the gal and go through the crib now myself; but
then she's hout and got her sparks with her. Conti said

there was another voman 'ere for the last week, and both vore lots 'o sparks, and never a man about the 'ouse Vy the job vill be so heasy that it von't be excitin'. [*Looks out again.*] Hi can see the guv'nor hin the shadow hof the vall hover the vay. What a magnificent willan that chap his. [*Hearing sound, steps inside, hurriedly closes window together, draws curtain aside and poses extravagantly at window, looking out.* 'Ow beautiful is the voice of natur' in this sylvian spot. [*Coming down.*] [*Kitty re-enters L. with glass of water*] I was a listenin for the vistle of the black-bird

Kitty. Here's the water, Mr.——

Jim. Bilkins,—Theopolis Bilkins, President of the society for the Propagation of the Heathen in furrin parts. [*Takes glass.*] There's nothing so good for the youthful blood as a glass hof sparkling water. [*Drinks, makes a wry face—aside.*] 'Ow I 'ates vater. [*Feeling in his pockets.*] I know what is due to a lady of your sex from a gentleman hof mine, and you shall have your reward. [*Still fumbling.*

Kitty. [*Curtsying and extending hand.*] Yes sir.

Jim. Hin the happroval of your conscience—a good conscience is a sweet thing. It's like grease to the boots, hit softens the huppers and makes the rough road of life come heasy. [BELL.] [*Door bell rings* R. U. E., *Jim starts.*

Kitty. Oh there's the missus—Oh murther !

Jim. Vich is the back vay out ?

Kitty. You must vait and see her, or she'll be thinking that I do be having a man here while she's away.

Jim. Hi can't vait, I must attend a meeting hof the Propagation Society. [BELL.] [*Bell rings again.*

Kitty. Oh my carracter, my carracter.

Jim. Vots your carracter, compared to mine ?

Kitty. Preachers are used to these things and I'm not. Don't you leave this room till the missus comes in. Stay right there now [BELL.] [*Bell rings again.*] Coming ma'am. The chickens will be gone now sure.

[*Runs of* R. U. E.

Jim. Stay here ? not hif hi knows it. I wonder where this door goes to. [L. U. E.] Hit must lead hinto the garden. I'll try. I 'opes there aint no daugs. [*exit* L. 2 E. KITTY *re-enters preceding* MRS. MONTAGUE, RITTA, SIR RANDALL *and* O'PAFF, *all in full opera dress, with wraps and overcoats, opera hats, etc.*

Kitty. [*Aside.*] Why the preacher's gone.

O'Paff. Ah, this is warm and cozy.

Mrs. Montague. The fire is pleasant after the nipping night air. Now make yourself at home, everybody. Kitty assist me.

Sir Randall. Allow me. [*He takes her opera cloak, passing it to Kitty.*]

Mrs. Montague. Thank you.

O'Paff. Ritta dear let me be your waiting maid.

Ritta. I fear you would not like it at all times.

O'Paff. I'm willing to engage on trial

[*Loud, coarse bark like a bull dog's bark off* L. U. E.

Kitty. [R., *Aside.*] O murther? The dog has the preacher.

Mrs. Montague. Kitty, is Nero loose?

Kitty. I think he be's ma'am.

O'Paff. Well, Nero's bark is untied at all events.

Kitty. Will ye's have a lunch ma'am? There's a bottle of wine and some cold fowl right handy ma'am.

Mrs. Montague. No, thank you, we lunched at the Brunswick.

Sir Randall. But we thank you for the hospitable intention all the same, Kitty.

O'Paff. She can't help it, she's Irish, and she's proud of it.

Kitty. Faith! I am. [*Aside.*] Oh he's a foine man, and he came from Dublin too. [*Exit* KITTY R. I E., *with wraps.*

Mrs. Montague. Ritta dear, I hope you have enjoyed the evening.

Ritta. [*Enthusiastically.*] Oh yes! so much! so much! no words can tell how much. I never heard *music* before.

O'Paff. Yes, you have dear, whenever you speak you hear it. [*Aside.*] Or I do.

Ritta. Oh when Patti sings I close my eyes and tink I hear all around me, de nightingale.

[SIR RANDALL *and* MRS. MONTAGUE *are* R. *by fire-place.*

O'Paff. That's what I used to fancy dear, when I heard you warbling your quaint little Italian airs. I observed one peculiarity, Ritta, that you must overcome.

Ritta. In me; what was it?

O'Paff. You seemed absorbed in the music—listened with wrapped attention, and applauded in the proper places.

Ritta. Was not that right?

O'Paff I dare say it was natural, dear, but it's not considered the correct thing. In order to appear fashionable at the opera, you must pay no attention to the music, but stare about you with languid indifference as though the whole thing were a bore. A little animated conversation during the pianissimo passages will also add to your prestige. [*All laugh.*]

Mrs. Montague. You are too severe, Mr. O'Paff, all theatre-goers are not vulgarians.

O'Paff. The amendment is accepted, though we must admit that the minority is a very aggressive one.

Sir Randall. O'Paff, old boy, you've become thoroughly Americanized, I fear.

O'Paff. I hope so.

Sir Randall. You're very severe on the aristocracy.

O'Paff. You're wrong, Sir Randall. There is but one aristocracy in America—the aristocracy of moral purity and intellectual worth. These qualities I admire, if I don't at all times emulate them. My reflections were directed at the *money*stocracy, a distinction with a difference.

Ritta. Well, I listen and applaud, because I love the music.

Mrs. Montague. And flowers, Ritta.

Ritta. [*Looking at her bouquet.*] Oh yes and flowers, and pictures, and everything that is beautiful, and the world is full of beautiful things, is it not, my dear good friend? [*taking* O'PAFF'S *hands affectionately.*

O'Paff. [*Looking into her face.*] Yes, dear it is, although I had'nt noticed so much until lately.

Ritta. [*Enthused.*] Oh to me, each flower, each scene, each new day is more beautiful than the last and some time I think it is too beautiful to be real, and that it is all a dream.

O'Paff. [*With serio comic tone.*] I've been feeling that way myself dear, lately. I hope no blackguard will come along and wake me.

Ritta. [*Jumping up.*] Oh! how bright the moon shines !
[*Goes up to window* C.

O'Paff. [*Following her up.*] Yes, dear. It's the kind of night we'd be sliding down hill, if we were only a little boy and girl again.

Ritta. [*In window.*] Can't we be children again, just for to-night ?

[RITTA *and* O'PAFF *stand in window—the moonlight falling on them.*]

Sir Randall. [*Looking at figures in window.*] Happy souls! See Helen, the moonlight blends their two shadows into one.

Mrs. Montague. I see. Alas! True love often lurks amid shadows!

Sir Randall. True, but the sunshine is always behind, ready to break through.

Mrs. Montague. [*Sadly.*] Not always.

Sir Randall. [*Tenderly.*] Dear Helen, your shadows will depart, whatever they may be, if you but bid them.

Mrs. Montague I fear not. I fear not.

Sir Randall. Then give me the right to drive them away.

Mrs. Montague. Believe me, I am honest when I say, I would if you could, but it is impossible.

Sir Randall. To the man and woman who honestly and truly loves, nothing is impossible.

Mrs Montague. [*Almost in tears.*] You cannot dream of what my sorrow consists, or you would see how hopeless is my future. Do not press me further, to-night.

[RITTA *and* O'PAFF *come forward.*

Ritta. And you really think you have a clue?

O'Paff. I know it dear, and a very important one.

Mrs. Montague. Have you any late developments in the case, Mr. O'Paff?

O'Paff. In a general way, yes. I have a skillful officer at work on the case in London and expect something definite at an early day.

Sir Randall. By the way, O'Paff, when does your partnership with Mr. Sawyer, go into effect.

O'Paff. Papers were signed to-day. From to-morrow morning the firm will be "Sawyer and O'Paff."

Ritta. Oh how can I ever repay you, repay all my loving friends for so much kindness to a poor lost child like me.

O'Paff. By saying nothing about it, dear, besides you're not lost, you're found. Think what our little group would have lost, had we never known the joy of your girlish presence, or felt the sunlight of your merry smile.

Ritta. You are so kind to say so, oh, could I ever hope that I might in some way repay you.

O'Paff You can dear with interest and a bonus.

Ritta. Oh tell me how, it shall be done.

O'Paff. You're sure you would'nt regret the promise.

Ritta. Quite sure, no matter what, tell me.

O'Paff. Well dear, I will.

Ritta. [*Eagerly looking up in his face.*] Yes!

O'Paff. Some other time, dear. [O'PAFF x's L. *and sits on piano stool.* RITTA *follows and stands beside him.*]

Ritta. You were going to tell me something. What was it? Ought I not to know?

O'Paff. [*Turning over music.*] I think you'll soon guess it, dear.

Ritta. I will guess it! Oh, when?

O'Paff. When you sing me this song, dear.

Ritta. Which one?

O'Paff This one. [*Plays prelude to song.*

Ritta. And then I shall know?

O'Paff. Yes!

RITTA *Sings ballad, accompanied by* O'PAFF; SIR RANDALL *and* MRS. MONTAGUE, *form picture in moonlight in bow window.*

Mrs. Montague. Thank you, Ritta dear, for your fitting finale to our evening of song.

O'Paff. Come Sir Randall, let's be off while the music still lingers in our ears.

[RITTA *gets* O'PAFF's *overcoat and assists him.*

Sir Randall. [*Taking* MRS. MONTAGUE's *hand* R.] Believe me, Helen, should circumstances arise to alter your determination, and make me your champion, you can rely upon my absolute devotion, no matter what the sacrifice may be, [*Kisses her hand.*] good night.

Mrs. Montague. Good night, dear friend.

[SIR RANDALL *goes up and gets coat.*

O'Paff. Ritta dear, you'd make a capital valet. Good night, sweet heart.

Ritta. [*Taking both his hands.*] Good night my dearest friend, my champion, *my brother.* [O'PAFF's *face brightens during her speech, and falls when she says "brother."*]

O'Paff. [*Serio-comic air.*] Good night, dear. [*To Mrs Montague.*] Good night, my dear friend. Ritta dear remember, that Saturday we visit the art galleries.

Ritta. [*Grieved surprise.*] Oh but shall I not see you to-morrow?

O'Paff. [*Pleased.*] Yes, dear, you shall.

Ritta. I must, I must see you every day.

O'Paff. You shall dear, a half dozen times a day. I'm with you, Sir Randall.

SIR RANDALL *and* O'PAFF, *exit pleasantly* R. U. E., *saying
"good night."* RITTA *kissing her hand to them.*

Ritta. [*Looking off* R.] Good night, my noble protector,
my brave hero! good night.

Mrs. Montague. [*At fire-place* R. *Aside.*] Dear child,
how happy she is! Heaven grant that no blight or shadow
may ever cross her young life.

[MRS MONTAGUE *taps table gong. Enter* KITTY R. I. E.
Kitty you can bolt the front door and then you may retire.

Kitty. Yes ma'am, thank ye ma'am. [*Exit* KITTY R. U. E.

Mrs. Montague. [*Aside.*] How noble and generous he is!
Oh the shame that my young life should be so clouded.

Ritta. [*Coming down.*] He is so handsome and noble,
Sir Randall.　　　　　　　　　　　　　　　[*Sits at her feet.*

Mrs. Montague. Now Ritta dear, tell me something of
yourself, your studies and how you progress at school.

Ritta. I am progressing famously, so all of my teachers say.

Mrs. Montague. And you like to study?

Ritta. Oh yes indeed. Each book and each lesson has
for me a separate charm. I was so long deprived of such
advantages. Only to think that I am but one year at school,
and I have learned so much. I am living in a new, strange
and beautiful world, a world where every hand seems
stretched out to protect me, instead of to beat me, and every
face greets me with sweet and welcome smiles.

Mrs. Montague. Then you have made many friends at
school?

Ritta. Oh yes I think every one is my friend and all seem
to love me.

Mrs. Montague. Tell me, what are your earliest recollec-
tions? Are they all associated with the Italian and his
cruelty?

Ritta. Yes, all.

Mrs. Montague. And you have no remembrance of a
mother?

Ritta. Sometimes I think I have. I seem to remember
as in a dream, a sweet face bending over me, and soft gentle
hands caressing me. It is like a vision, with large soft eyes
and golden hair, it smiles and kisses me, and then I wake
from my day dream, and in its place comes back the old
memories of cruelty, and misery.

Mrs. Montague. Poor child!

Ritta. Then I recall the hour when womanhood seemed to come to me so suddenly, and give me courage to rebel, and tell me that I was not born for such a fate, then the desperate struggle between the strong man and the weak girl, the cloud for a moment darkens around me, but in that moment Heaven's angel of deliverance stands in the door.

Mrs. Montague. And then?

Ritta. And then your own sweet face and gentle voice comes into my new life, to remain a part of it I hope forever.

Mrs. Montague. I hope so, my child, although mine is but a second claim upon you. Mr. O'Paff, who brought you to me, has determined to solve the mystery of your birth, and it is to him and not to me that you owe your education and the luxuries that have surrounded you.

Ritta. Oh, I did not know that.

Mrs. Montague. I know it, dear, and possibly I have done wrong in telling you.

Ritta. Oh no, I think it was right that I should know.

Mrs. Montague. And Mr. O'Paff has given you no hint as to his plans for your future?

Ritta. No, he writes often to me, and always cheerfully, encourages me in my studies, and sends me books to read during my leisure hours.

Mrs. Montague. And nothing else?

Ritta. Is not that enough?

Mrs. Montague. [*Aside.*] Generous hearted fellow! He worships this child, yet shrinks from winning her through her sense of gratitude.

Ritta. And now dear Mamma Montague, may I call you mamma?

Mrs. Montague. Do I shall like it of all things.

Ritta. Well then dear mamma, now that we have talked so much about myself, let us talk of a more worthy subject.

Mrs. Montague. Of what?

Ritta. Of yourself and your noble solicitor Sir Randall, when may I congratulate you?

Mrs. Montague. I fear that time will never come, Ritta dear.

Ritta. Not marry him! oh why?

Mrs. Montague. [*Kissing* Ritta's *forehead.*] Hush! my child! not now, not now. [*Conceals her face for a moment, nearly weeping, then recovers and assumes a cheerful manner.*]

Ritta dear, there is a shadow in my life as in your own; a shadow that stands between Sir Randall Burns and myself. Feeling that I loved him, I have not had the heart to tell

him the truth.   Indeed the secret is my own, and it is one
that often weighs heavily upon me.

Ritta. May I not share it dear mamma ?

Mrs. Montague. I have been thinking to-night dear, that
I should feel better in mind and heart, could I unbosom
myself to you.   The load is growing too heavy for me to
bear alone.

Ritta. Please let me share the burden, you shall find me
worthy of your confidence.

Mrs. Montague. I will my child, and should you ever be
tempted to disregard the wishes of those who cherish you,
let my sad story warn you of your danger.   When a school
girl, a mere child like yourself, there crossed my path a
tempter in the shape of one who seemed to my girlish fancy
all that was noble, handsome and chivalrous.   Blinded by a
foolish passion, I set at naught a parent's teaching, and deaf
to the counsels of friends, I took into my heart this idol of
clay, surrounding it with a false halo of romance.   I awoke
from my dream when it was too late, and a life of misery
and penitence has been my punishment for the folly of an
hour.   [*She weeps.*

Ritta. Poor mamma ! he deserted you ?

Mrs. Montague. No child, but upon the day of my
marriage I learned that he was a miserable criminal, he came
of a good family whom he had disgraced, and by whom he
had been cast off.   His pretended wealth and titles were lies,
and his only object in marrying me was to secure my fortune.   In this, however he was thwarted, and in my bridal
robes I fled from his presence.

Ritta. And you have never seen him since ?

Mrs. Montague. Not for years   He followed me to London, and began a series of persecutions, until he was detected
in some great crime, which relieved me of his presence.   I
have not seen him since, and know not whether he be living
or dead.

Ritta. Ah now I can understand why you are sometimes
so sad.

Mrs. Montague. Yes child. It is that I am never free of the
haunting fear that he will find me out and renew his persecutions.   But there, Ritta dear, forgive me for having brought
tears into those beautiful eyes ; your sweet face should reflect
nothing but smiles.   Come dear we must retire.   It is almost
midnight.

Ritta. I don't like to say good night while you are so sad. [*Putting arm around her.*] I'll go to your room, kiss you good night there, then return to my own.

Mrs. Montague. Thank you dear.

Exit RITTA *and* MRS. MONTAGUE, R. I. E., RITTA *after turning down light on table. Music. Lights two-thirds down; window at back gradually opens and* JIM'S *head is seen, he cautiously enters through the window, now in his shirt sleeves. He peeps around the room, then comes down* C. *he has a bull's eye lamp, and a small revolver.*

Jim. Oh, but I 'ates daugs. [*His clothes are badly torn, and rags hanging from seat of trousers.*]

I seed the light go hout, and says to myself " haul right," my pippin, the ladies is snug in bed. [*Runs up to window.*] There's the Capting in the shadow of the vall. Vot a manificent villian he is? [*Comes down* C.] Let me see, the Captain said I vos first to get the *hexact* locality of the room vere the voman sleeps, then I was to hunfasten the front door— Old Conti says the voman vore a necklace of sparks as must 'av been vorth a cool thousand—The Capting vont crib nothink but sparks, he vont, I haint so bloomin' particular, I haint. [*Looks through archway* L.

There's a bed and no von hin it. [*Peeps off* R., *listens at door* R. I. E.] I can 'ear 'em a chinnin' in there, that's the werry hidentical room. While they're going to sleep, I'll see vot I can pick hup in a small vay on my hown haccount. *Runs up to dressing case in* R. *arch, examines toilet articles, opens drawers examining them by light of his bull's eye, he pulls out clothes, small boxes and bundles, fills his arms full, turns into room.*

Vy I've got enough to hopen a shop. [*Dog barks off* L. U. E., JIM *drops everything, a picture of comic fright.*] 'Ow I 'ates daugs. [*Gathers up the articles and is in a quandary as to what he will do with them.*] Vere can I put 'em, me pocket vont 'old em. [*Sees umbrella in hallway* R.

A humbrella! The werry blessed think!

[*Runs and gets umbrella, is greatly bothered between the bundles, his pistol, bull's eye, umbrella, &c.*] Ive got to get rid of somethink.

[*Lays his pistol on table* R., *sits down and crams things into the inverted umbrella, then runs up to toilet case* R. *again and crowds in laces, stockings, &c. Ad lib.*]

Hoppera glasses! and ere's a vatch, I wonder vere the bloomin' chain is. [*Rams his head into a drawer up to his shoulders.* RITTA *enters* R. I. E. *Lights up gradually.*]

Ritta. [*Looking back.*] O good night, my sweet mamma.

Mrs. Montague. [*Off* R.] Good night, Ritta my child and happy dreams to you.

RITTA *turns up* C. *as though going to her room, sees* JIM *at toilet case, she sees* JIM *turn up light on table and in doing so, sees* JIM'S *revolver, which she takes up resolutely.*

Jim. [*Coming down* L. C.] I'll chuck the bloomin' umbrella out o' the vinder, and hopen the front door for the Capting. [*Turns up* R. C. *and* RITTA *shoves the pistol into his face.* PICTURE.

Jim. Vy I know that face—

Ritta. [*recognizing* JIM.] What Jim! what are you doing here?

Jim. [*Gasping.*] S'elp me Bob its Conti's kid.

Ritta. Has Conti sent you to search me out?

Jim. Vy no Miss Ritta, I vos on a little henterprise of my own miss, and I-I-s'elp me! I didn't know as ow *you* vas 'ere.

Ritta. I ought to give you up, but I've not forgotten that you often befriended me. Do not alarm or frighten *her*, go quickly for my sake.

Jim. I'll go for my own—'ow shall I go?

Ritta. [*Pointing to* L. 2 E.] That way, I will let you out through the kitchen.

Jim. [*His mind on the dog.*] Can't I go out the front way?

JASPER CRADDOCK *comes rapidly through the window, takes in situation and rushes down* C.

Ritta. No, you might be observed, go that way.

Jasper. [*Taking pistol from* RITTA.] Pardon me, your hand is too delicate.

[MRS. MONTAGUE *enters* R. I. E., *rapidly.*

Mrs. Montague. [*Speaking as she enters.*] Who are these men? Burglars?

[CRADDOCK *turns quickly at sound of her voice, starts.*

PICTURE.

Jasper. Helen Montague!

Mrs. Montague. My God! You here!

SIR RANDALL *enters through window, speaking rapidly as he comes down.*

Sir Randall. Returning from O'Paff's lodgings to my hotel, I saw this man entering by that window, and hastened to follow him.

Jasper. [*Recovering his composure.*] Indeed! Possibly you will have the politeness to return as you came.

Sir Randall. [*Seizes him by the shoulder.*] Yes sir, and I'll trouble you to accompany me.

Jasper. [*Removing* SIR RANDALL's *hand.*] You are mistaken my good man, I shall remain.

Sir Randall. Remain! By what right?

Jasper. [*Coolly.*] By the right of a husband.

Sir Randall. [*Astonished.*] A husband?

Jasper. Yes, *her* husband, let her deny it if she dare.

Mrs. Montague. Heaven help me! He speaks the truth.
                [*Sinks on floor burying her face in sofa* R.

Ritta. Her husband!

RING.

[JIM *is on piano stool* L., *a picture of wild consternation.*

ENCORE.

RITTA *is kneeling at feet of* MRS. MONTAGUE, R. SIR RANDALL *and* CRADDOCK, *looking defiantly at each other,* L. 2 E. JIM *with his umbrella starts to sneak out at window, just as he reaches it* HOFFMEIER *appears at window,* JIM *rolls back into room, falling* C.

Jim. Her husbing! great 'Eavings. [*Raises his umbrella and is buried in a shower of laces, stockings, trinkets, &c.*]

RING.

ACT IV.

SCENE I.—*Law office of* SAWYER & O'PAFF, C. D., *open backed by library piece or book case. Boxed scene. Practical doors* R. 2 E. *and* L. 2 F., *in boxing walls all painted into book cases, &c. in various designs. The office is that of a rich and respectable firm.* R. *door hung so as to swing both ways. When it opens into room, the exterior exposes the sign of the firm on the door, viz:*

SAWYER & O'PAFF,

Attorneys-at-Law.

Transom over door R., *contains same sign and imitation glass, reading backwards to the audience. Large imitation transom over* C. *doors with same sign. Large office desks* R. *and* L., *table tops, baize covered, arched opening in* C., *with drawers down the sides, (regular office table desks.) Safe at back* R. *Letter-press on top of safe* R. *Revolving office chairs at desks. Other chairs* R. *and* L., *all of the appurtenances of a completely equipped law office.*
Crane, the clerk, comes through C. D., *with large assortment of letters, which he is examining, and during speech, places them alternately on the desks* R. *and* L.

Crane. A large mail this morning. [*Reads.*] "Sawyer, personal," that goes here. [R.] "Sawyer & O'Paff," ditto, ditto, ditto. [*Placing letters* R.] "Felix O'Paff," that goes here. [L.] London postmark! that must be what Mr. O'Paff has been so anxious about! Hello! here's another from London for Mr. Sawyer, [R] that's about the Craddock business. A great calling is our noble profession of the law! The junior partner is wonderfully active, he has infused new life into the firm. That London letter must be something about the little Italian girl, that Mr. O'Paff is so wonderfully interested in. [*Looks at watch.*] Nine o'clock, and there's Mr. Sawyer's step, as punctual as a tax collector.

[*Enter* SEPTIMUS SAWYER, R. 2 E.

Sawyer. Oh, good morning, Crane.

Crane. Good morning, sir.

Sawyer. O'Paff here yet?

Crane. Not yet, sir.

Sawyer. That's odd, he's usually first. [*Taking off coat, gloves, &c.*]

Crane. You forget that there is an attraction elsewhere just now, sir.

Sawyer. Eh! Attraction! Oh, yes, of course, his little Italian protege is home from school, I forgive him. Any mail, Crane? [*At desk* R.

Crane. Yes, sir, on your desk.

Sawyer. Anyone called?

Crane. Mr. Craddock, said he'd be back between nine and ten.

Sawyer. Indeed! And here, I take it, is something that may concern him, [*Sits and opens large letter.*] from our London agents, Podgers & Podgers. [*Reads.*

Mr. Septimus Sawyer, dear sir:

In regard to the claims of your client, Jasper Craddock, we must inform you that the Craddock estates were left to an infant niece of your client, in trust to her mother. The mother is known to be deceased, the child was reported as lost or stolen some fifteen years ago. Your client must establish the death of the heir, before he can hope to gain possession of his father's estates; otherwise it reverts to the crown. Let us know what further steps, you desire us to take.

Respectfully,

Podgers & Podgers.

That looks bad for Craddock, eh Crane?

Crane. Rather smoky.

Sawyer. Still, as my worthy junior, Mr. O'Paff, has discovered or thinks he has, that my client is one of the links in the chain of circumstantial evidence which he is forging, we must go gently, eh Crane?

Crane. Evidently.

Sawyer. Any mail for O'Paff?

Crane. Yes, sir, and a letter from the London authorities.

Sawyer. Indeed! In that case we must hold Craddock off until O'Paff has read his letters, you understand!

Crane. Perfectly, sir. Yes sir. Oh the great brain power that we require in our noble profession of the law.

[*Exit* CRANE R. 2 E.

Sawyer. I must confess that my junior partner brought two very charming clients into the firm. The lovely English widow and the bewitching little Italian are enough to make the reputation of a less talented man than O'Paff.

Crane. [*In* C. *door.*] He's here.

Sawyer. All right, keep your eye open.

[CRADDOCK *enters* C. D., CRANE *exits* R. C. *after bowing* CRADDOCK *in politely.*]

Sawyer. Ah, good morning, Mr. Craddock, I was just thinking about you, and wondering whether we should get anything for you to-day. Be seated. [CRADDOCK *sits* R. C.

Craddock. Thank you. Is it possible you have nothing from London yet?

Sawyer. I think not. [*Calls.*] Crane. [CRANE *appears in* C. D.] No later mails this morning?

Crane. Nothing later, no sir.

Sawyer. I thought not. [CRANE *disappears* R. C.

Craddock. It seems to me that you have had sufficient time to have heard something.

Sawyer. Yes, it does look that way. Podgers & Podgers are a little slow and old fogyish perhaps, possibly we could hurry matters up by retaining a more pushing firm, say, "Sharp & Short," of Chancery Lane, they're younger and livelier.

Craddock. Then why not have retained them in the first place? do so at once. The last firm that I retained to look this matter up, dilly-dallied a year or so without learning anything, that's why I have come to you.

Sawyer. Quite right, served 'em right. Oh, I'll work it up for you. Well, now, what shall we say as a retainer for Sharp & Short?

Craddock. Why whatever is customary. The property belongs to me, I know my father is dead, my sister and her child are dead, and I will have what is my own.

Sawyer. Quite right, well, suppose we say two hundred dollars for Sharp & Short, of Chancery Lane?

Craddock. Very well, there are four fifties. [*Gives money to* SAWYER.] And now I want to consult you upon another point, can a man compel his wife to live with him?

Sawyer. Well, that's a poser. He *might persuade* her, but as for compelling, *that's different.* Wife in this country ?

Craddock. Yes, in this city.

Sawyer. And refuses to live with her husband ?

Craddock. Refuses to *see* him, has even invoked special police protection.

Sawyer. That looks as though she meant business.

Craddock. Well, can't he compel her to share with him their ample means ?

Sawyer. Her money or his ?

Craddock. Well, hers, I suppose.

Sawyer. Well with my limited knowledge of the case, and my extended knowledge of American jurisprudence, I should say that the lady has rather the inside track up to the present time.

Craddock. Is there no law to sustain a man in insisting upon his conjugal rights.

Sawyer. Well, that's another poser, I shall have to look that thing up. I'd like to consult my partner upon that point, he's a wonderful man on technicalities. Suppose you call around in half an hour.

Craddock. Oh, very well.

Sawyer. By that time we shall doubtless have another mail, and possibly something about your London matter.

Craddock. Ah exactly. I've some business at my banker's in the adjoining street, after which I'll drop in again.

CRANE *appears quickly in* C. D., *gives a quick motion to* SAWYER *to signify that some one is coming, and exits* C. CRADDOCK *during above action is buttoning his coat, or glove, so as not to see it, it is but an instant.* CRADDOCK *starts up* C.

Sawyer. Ah, Mr. Craddock, you'll find this a more direct exit. [*Pointing* R. 2. E.

Craddock. Oh indeed ! thank you, [x'ing *to* R.] good morning. [*Exit* R. 2 E.

Sawyer. Good morning. Business at his banker's ! referring doubtless to some disciple of King *Faro*, that fellow is a cool hand, confounded blackguard ! [*Folding up money, and placing it in vest pocket*] I'm afraid, Mr. Craddock, that you will have to charge this retainer for Sharp & Short, to profit and loss. [O'PAFF *and* RITTA *enter* C. D.

O' Paff. Come in, Ritta dear, don't be frightened, they call us lawyers, sharks and wolves and other pet names, but we're only flesh and blood like other people.

Top o' the morning to ye, Mr. Sawyer. Sit down dear.
[*Gives* RITTA *chair* R.] Excuse me while I look over my
letters.

Sawyer. Good morning, Miss Ritta.

Ritta. Good morning, Mr Sawyer, why, what a nice,
bright office you have !

O'Paff. Yes dear, its a part of the plot to make the
wolves' den attractive to the eye, to lure the victim to his
fate.   [*All laugh.* O'PAFF *reading lettters.*

Sawyer. How are you enjoying your vacation, Miss Ritta ?

Ritta. Oh wonderfully !   We all attended the opera last
night.

Sawyer. Oh yes, I saw you.

Ritta. And were you there ?   I did not see you.

Sawyer. Oh no, you were too absorbed in the music ; oh
yes, I was there.

O'Paff. Yes, Sawyer had a front seat in the orchestra.
He left when the ballet was over.   [*All laugh.*

Sawyer. And when do you return to school, Miss Ritta ?

Ritta. It is not decided. My guardian, Mrs. Montague,
is very anxious for me to visit London with her, as soon as
her affairs are settled here.

O'Paff. [*Who has been examining London letter.*] Well
her affairs promise to be settled sooner than we thought.
Here's my letter from Inspector Fields, of Scotland Yards,
listen—   [*Reads.*

" Felix O'Paff, Esq., New York City.

   Dear sir :

In looking up the record of your man, Jasper Craddock,
we have found that just one year prior to his marriage with
your client, he had married a Miss Julia Green, a daughter
of one of his father's tenants. I enclose a bit of documentary evidence. No publicity was given to the marriage,
but the wife and her child were still living at the time he
married your client, Miss Helen Montague, in St. Paul's
Church, at Bath, this is authentic, your client, has never been
the wife of Jasper Craddock."

Ritta. Then dear mamma Montague, is free ?

O'Paff. As free as air, dear.

Ritta. Oh what joyous news for her. And now you will
give this villian up to justice at once ?

O'Paff. Oh no dear, that would be spoiling sport. We've hooked the fish, but he's a big one, and we must play with him until he drowns himself.

Ritta. But this evidence seems decisive.

O'Paff. So it is, dear, as far as Mrs. Montague is concerned, but that is but the beginning of the end. There's another case involved.

Ritta. Another case ?

O'Paff. Yes, child, *your own.* Listen to the rest of the London officer's letter— [*Reads.*

" Young Craddock seems to have been a very bad one, so bad in fact, that his father, who was a man of great wealth, ignored him in his will, leaving the entire estates, to an infant daughter of young Craddock's sister, in trust to the mother who was a confirmed invalid. Shortly after the father's death, the child was lost or stolen, and the death of the mother soon followed. This was fourteen years ago, and the child has never since been seen or heard of. Suspicion fell upon the brother and an Italian of the criminal classes known as Paulo Viotti, but before the chain of evidence could be completed, young Craddock was arrested for complicity in the famous Lady Danforth diamond robbery, and sentenced to Australia, for fifteen years. The Italian Viotti disappeared simultaneously, and all trace of him has been lost."

You see now, how nicely one thing fits into the other, as the cords begin to tighten.

Sawyer. That certainly begins to look as though you were on the right track.

Ritta. And does this concern me ?

O'Paff. Very nearly, my dear. Every circumstance points to you as the niece of Jasper Craddock and the heir to his father's estates.

Ritta. But this speaks of an Italian named *Paulo Viotti.*

O'Paff. Exactly, my dear. It's an easy thing to change one's name, but not so easy for us to prove it, and the burden of proof rests with us. But listen— [*Reads.*

" The child, Grace Mayberry, when stolen was suffering from a serious scald upon the left shoulder. [*Action of surprise from* RITTA.] The burn was a very severe one, and would doubtless leave a permanent scar. This is the only clue we have ever had, and our only means of fixing the girl's identity."

Ritta. [*Excitedly.*] I have such a scar on my left shoulder.

O'Paff. [*Jumps up.*] You have! I knew it.

[*Rushes towards her, as though to examine the scar, then suddenly stops.*]

Sawyer. [*Quickly, as* O'PAFF X's.] Good gracious, O'Paff!

O'Paff. Yes, certainly, of course you have dear, and did Conti never explain it to you?

Ritta. No, once as a child, I asked him how it came there, and he flew into a violent rage, saying it was a birth-mark, and that I must never refer to it again. He frightened me so that I never did.

O'Paff. The old reprobate!

Sawyer. Craddock will be here shortly.

O'Paff. True for you. By the way, Sawyer, please ask Crane to have my friend Hoffmeier call around, we're liable to need him this morning.

Sawyer. All right. I'll keep an eye open outside, and see that you are not interrupted.   [*Exit* SAWYER C. D.

O'Paff. Now, d'ye see, jewel, how I'm narrowing the circle of which your fairy little self is the centre.

Ritta. You are so good, so noble, so brave, but I feel so unworthy of all that you are doing for me.

O'Paff. But you mustn't feel that way, dear. I've simply done what any honest man would feel it a privilege to do under the circumstances. Lawyers sometimes have hearts, dear. This has been to me a labor of love, and one sweet smile repays me for services rendered to date, and the ripling music of one merry laugh would retain me in the case for the remainder of my days. [RITTA. *laughs.*] Does that laugh tell me that I am retained for life, dear?

Ritta. What am I that you have not made me? What have I that you have not given me? To give you my poor little self is not enough.

O'Paff. I'd be satisfied with it, dear, provided you don't give yourself through a mistaken sense of duty or gratitude.

Ritta. [*Modestly.*] Oh, no. It is something more than that I feel for you.

Oh but suppose I should be the Italian's child after all?

O'Paff. All of the rules of evidence are against the supposition.

Ritta. But I might be?

O'Paff. Then I'll take the case on its individual merits, dear. [SAWYER *appears* C. D., *sees their faces very close together, coughs and disappears.*] What's that?

Sawyer. [*Entering* C.] How about Sir Randall and the widow?

O'Paff. Let them come in, but hold Craddock off until I'm done with the other fellow.

Sawyer. All right. [*Exit* C., *as* SIR RANDALL *and* MRS MONTAGUE *enter.*]

O'Paff. My dear Mrs. Montague, you've arrived at a happy moment. Fate has been kind to us. See now how blessings often come to us in disguise, yours came in the shape of a burglar, disguised as a husband, and Sir Randall learned for himself the secret, you had not the courage to confide to him, and like the noble fellow that he is, he loved you more dearly as the clouds grew darker, and he invoked the aid of a legal angel in the person of Felix O'Paff, Esquire, who now has the happiness and the honor to inform you that you are a free woman, that you have never been the wife of Jasper Craddock, and here's some documentary evidence. [*Gives the letter to* MRS. MONTAGUE.] Come Ritta dear, step into the private consultation room, I'll show you the revised statutes and congressional reports. They're very thrilling. [*Passes* RITTA *off* L. 2 E.] What do you think of that, ma'am?

Mrs. Montague. Why I am astonished at this man's audacious villiany. I can find no words, Mr. O'Paff, to thank you for your skill and energy in my behalf.

O'Paff. Don't try, ma'am. The labor we delight in, physics pain. [*Aside to* SIR RANDALL.] Now's your time, make hay while the iron's hot, I mean, strike while the sun shines, no, I mean, never do to-morrow what you can put off until to-day. [*Exit* O'PAFF L. 2 E.

Sir Randall. And now, Helen, since the shadows that haunted you have been dispelled, what have you to say to me?

Mrs. Montague. Sir Randall, I will not pretend that I do not understand you, but ask you to defer the subject to a fitter time and place.

Sir Randall. Why, Helen, any place, even a lawyer's office, could scarcely be objectional to the solving of a question that's to make a fellow happy or miserable for life.

Mrs. Montague. Well, Randall, now that I am really free, I cannot but acknowledge your devotion to my interests, and I candidly confess to you that if I have not given you the encouragement you desired, it was no fault of my heart. I sincerely hope you are not mistaken in your feelings.

Sir Randall. [*Taking both her hands.*] If the devotion of my life to you will be a proof that I am not mistaken I tender it. Will you accept the unworthy offering?

Mrs. Montague. You would be angry if I said no, so what can I say? [*Enter* O'PAFF L. 2 E.

O'Paff. Say nothing at all, silence gives consent, only say it in the private consultation room here.

[SIR RANDALL *and* MRS. MONTAGUE *hurry off* L. 2 E. *laughing.* SAWYER *appears in* C. *door.*]

Sawyer. I say, O'Paff, it seems to me that you are converting this office into a "Lover's Retreat."

O'Paff. Not at all, I'm enlarging our sphere of usefulness by adding a matrimonial agency.

Sawyer. Well, where does the senior partner come in?

O'Paff. The senior partner don't come in, he gets left. See here, Sawyer, you waited too long.

Sawyer. I believe I did. If I had my life to live over again, damme! I'd marry at twenty.

[CRANE *appears hurriedly in* C. *door* R.

Crane. Your man is here.

O'Paff. Good. Send him in the other way.

Crane. The other way goes. [*Exit* CRANE R. C.

Sawyer. I'll be within ear shot. [*Exit* C. D. L.

O'Paff. [*Opens door* L. 2 E.; *calls.*] Sir Randall! [SIR RANDALL *appears in door* L. 2 E.] I want all to hear what passes in this room, but let no one enter till I call.

Sir Randall. All right. [SIR RANDALL *withdraws into room* L. 2 E.]

O'Paff. [*At his desk* L.] Ritta's fate is trembling in the balance. Ten minutes will confirm my hopes or baffle my plot, the London letter arrived just in time. [*Knock on door* R. 2 E.] Ah, he's there! Now for a breeze or a hurricane. [*Knock on door* R. 2 E.] Come in.

O'PAFF *absorbed with his writing.* CONTI *slouches sullenly into the room,* R. 2 E. *and stands* R. C. *scowling.*

O'Paff. Ah, Mr. Conti, is it yourself? You're punctual, sit down.

Conti. What for you send a de polichaman for me? What you want wid a me?

O'Paff. Well friend Conti, I hadn't seen you in so long that I feared you had forgotten my address, so I told our mutual friend Hoffmeier to invite you around. Sit down, Mr. Conti, don't be bashful.

Conti. [*Dropping into chair* R. C.] Well, me a here. What you want wid a me? You ought to be ashamed to meet wid a man when you steal a his child from him.

O'Paff. Why, Mr. Conti, you've grown sensitive. Were you always troubled with such fine feelings?

Conti. Got as much a fine a feel as a lawyer.

O'Paff. Thank ye for the compliment. By the way, Mr. Conti, [*Abruptly.*] where's Ritta's mother?

Conti. [*Starting.*] Ritta moder! She a dead.

O'Paff. How do you know that?

Conti. How I know? Me see her when she die.

O'Paff. Were you in London?

Conti. [*Start.*] London! No! she die in Italy.

O'Paff. You're mistaken, Mr. Conti. Ritta's mother did not die in Italy.

Conti. [*Start bus.*] Not in Italy?

O'Paff. [*Aside.*] That was a random shot, but it hit the bull's eye.

Conti. *You* are a mistake. I was a dare.

O'Paff. I make no mistakes, if I do I'll stick to them. Ritta's mother died in London, I was there, [CONTI *starts*] that's another. [*Aside.*] Where's her father?

Conti. [*Half frightened, but defiantly.*] Her fader! here, in dis a chair. Me, Giovanni Conti, me a her a fader.

O'Paff. Giovanni Conti is Ritta's father?

Conti. Si.

O'Paff. Then you can't be her father. For *you are Paulo Viotti.*

Conti. [*Starts in fright.*] Me! No, no! Who tell a you? [*Recovering.*] No, you are a mistake, me, Giovanni Conti.

O'Paff. Just now you are. Mr. Conti, you may as well make a clean breast of it, and save yourself while you have a chance. Cockney Jim has given the game away, and the old crone, Rosa, has turned against you. The old mantel has revealed its stolen treasure, and I can give you five years as a receiver of stolen goods. You may as well confess.

Conti. [*Doggedly.*] Confess! Confess a what? you are
a mistake. If dey find a de stolen goods, it was a de ole
woman, not a me, I work a, I grind a de org for my live, me
got a noting to confess,

O'Paff. [*Aside.*] The old devil is a cute one, I'll try the
other game. [*Aloud.*] Mr. Conti, if you will tell me the
truth about the girl Ritta, I'll guarantee you immunity from
prosecution, and pay you more than you can hope to gain
by your present course.

Conti. [*Aside, gloating savagely.*] Aha! he know noting!
he only guess, he tink he frighten me. He try to pump a
me, aha! [*Aloud.*] Me tell a you de truth, me have a no
more to tell. [*Rising.*] Ritta my child. You steal a her
from me, and now you try to frighten me, to make a me,
disown my own child. [*Getting savage.*] You not a
frighten me, me no fool, me hard-working citizen, you give
a me my child. [*Approaches* O'PAFF *threateningly.*] Me
go to de Mayor, de Judge, me invoke a de law. De Italian
got a some a right in dis a country, de same as de Irishman.
Me have a no more a bull a doza from you. [*Slapping
desk.*] I demand a from you my child!

O'Paff. Don't get excited, Mr. Conti. By the way when
did you last see your friend, *Jasper Craddock?*

Conti. [*Starts.*] Ha! Jasper Craddock! Not a my friend.
Me don't a know such a man as Jasper Craddock.

O'Paff. [*Aside.*] He's my man. [*Aloud.*] Mr. Conti,
I'm afraid you have a bad memory. I'll give you thirty
minutes in which to freshen it. Return in that time with
the truth on your tongue, or by Heaven! I'll give you ten
years in Sing Sing, and when you've done that I'll turn you
over to the tender mercies of the British Government, and
let them deal with you for abduction. Now, go.

[O'PAFF *goes to writing.* CONTI X's *sullenly to* R., *then
comes back to* O'PAFF'S *desk.*]

Conti. How much you give a me to let Ritta go.

 O'Paff. Nothing. I've got her.   [CONTI *starts* R.]
Stop! Come back in half an hour with a truthful answer
to my question, and I'll give you your freedom to leave the
country, which is more than you deserve. Go! [CONTI X's
R.] And don't try to escape, or to communicate with your
friends, for from this time forth you're walking in the shadow

of the law, and there's an eye upon you at every corner as you pass. [CONTI *edges over to door* R. 2 E., *and hits it savagely.*]

Conti. [*As passes out, looking back.*] Damn a de lawyer.

[*Exit* R. 2 E.

[O'PAFF *beckons* C., HOFFMEIER *comes on* C. D., *and goes off* R. 2 E., *following* CONTI.]

O'Paff. He's my man.

Sawyer. [*Entering* C. D.] Without a doubt.

O'Paff. But how to prove it, and to get the connecting link between himself and Craddock. If they are working together here, they are playing mighty cleverly into each other's hands.

Sawyer. What's the next move?

O'Paff. We must make them convict themselves.

Sawyer. Easily said, but how?

O'Paff. By getting them at loggerheads, or trapping one or the other of them into a confession.

Sawyer. They are both sharp rascals. Do you think the Italian will weaken?

O'Paff. Devil a bit. He's cleverer than I thought.

Sawyer. It's time for Craddock, what shall we do with him?

O'Paff. Leave him to me. I'll play with him a while and then drown him. [*Enter* CRANE C. *quickly.*

Crane. The first heavy villian is returning.

Exit CRANE C. O'PAFF *and* SAWYER *both at their desks, apparently absorbed. Enter* CRADDOCK R. C. *goes down* R. C.

Sawyer. Oh, Mr. Craddock, we were just speaking of you.

Craddock. [*Pleasantly.*] Nothing to my discredit I hope.

Sawyer. Quite the contrary. By the way, Mr. Craddock, this is my partner, Mr. O'Paff.

Craddock. Delighted, I'm sure.

O'Paff. Same to yourself, sir.

Craddock. I was not aware until this morning that Mr. Sawyer had an active partner.

O'Paff. No sir, I became a member of the firm subsequent to your retaining my worthy senior.

Craddock. I knew that I had not met you.

O'Paff. The pleasure was mutual, sir.

Craddock. Eh!

O'Paff. Be seated, sir.

Craddock. Thank you. [*Sits* R.] Perhaps I have returned too soon?

Sawyer. Oh no.

O'Paff. Just in time, sir.

Craddock. Anything about my affairs by the last mail?

Sawyer. [*Writing*] Well, I've been rather busy since you went out. Mr. O'Paff, I believe, has a communication that may prove interesting.

Craddock. Oh indeed.

O'Paff. Yes I was wondering, Mr. Craddock, why you let so many years pass before claiming this estate.

Craddock. [*Annoyed.*] Why, I only recently learned of the death of my sister and her child. I have an independent property, and have passed many years traveling in India and Africa.

O'Paff. I'm something of a traveler myself, your face is familiar to me, I must have met you in Australia

Craddock. [*Annoyed.*] You're mistaken. I said I had been in Africa and India.

O'Paff. Certainly, of course. I must have met you nearer home. It was at Homburg, last Summer.

Craddock. I was not at Homburg, last Summer.

O'Paff. Then it must have been at Bath.

Craddock. [*Annoyed.*] I've frequently been at Bath.

O'Paff. Of course. At Homburg I was treating for my liver, and at Bath I had an attack of the kidneys, being near together I got the places confused.

Craddock. [*Aside.*] This fellow seems to be making game of me.

O'Paff. Now wouldn't you find it more expeditious to go personally to London?

Craddock. Possibly, but I have certain family reasons for not wishing to return to England, just at present.

O'Paff. Certainly, of course. By the bye, Mr. Haddock—

Craddock. *Crad*dock, if you've no objections.

O'Paff. None in the least, sir. I beg your pardon, I ought to remember the name, I had a client of the same name in Dublin, Four Courts, the year I was admitted. There was a will in his case too, he abstracted one, and the man died suddenly who tried to prevent him. I thought there was a similarity.

Craddock, Sir !

O'Paff. In the name. Well, sir, I pleaded for that man for nineteen straight hours, they gave him twenty years, and the jury were of the unanimous opinion, that if my voice had lasted another hour they'd have hung him.

Craddock. Yes, I dare say, but about the London agent's letter ?

O'Paff. Certainly, of course. Relating to your marriage Mr. Craddock, regarding which you consulted. Mr. Sawyer, were you married in England ?

Craddock. Certainly, at Bath.

O'Paff. At Bath of course. Were you married in church ?

Craddock. Certainly, St. Paul's Church.

O'Paff. Of course, St. Paul's. Were you married by St. Paul, I mean by the rector ?

Craddock. Certainly.

O'Paff. Were you ever married before ?

Craddock, [*Startled.*] Who said so ?—I—no, of course not.

O'Paff. I thought it might have slipped your memory.

Craddock. No, sir, my memory is too good.

O'Paff. That's why I asked. What was your wife's maiden name ?

Craddock. Why, Helen Montague.

O'Paff. Isn't your memory treacherous—

Craddock. [*Jumping up.*] See here, what are you driving at ?

O'Paff. I'm driving at you, Mr. Craddock.

Craddock. What does this mean ? I paid your senior here a liberal retainer to establish my title to my father's estates, and now instead of treating me with the courtesy due a client, you cross-examine and brow-beat me like a criminal. You were not employed as detectives to spy into my domestic life. I simply asked of you, the law.

O'Paff. Well ain't you getting all you want of it ?

Craddock. Is this what you call law here in America ?

O'Paff. It's what we call justice here in America, the terms are sometimes, but not always synonomous.

Craddock. [*Moving to door.*] Good morning.

O'Paff. Don't leave us in anger. I'll introduce you to some friends of mine. Come in ladies.

[*Enter* MRS. MONTAGUE, RITTA *and* SIR RANDALL, L. 2 E.] [CRADDOCK *starts—pause.*] Mrs. Montague, I thought possibly you might want to take a farewell look at your ex-lord and master.

Mrs. Montague Mr. O'Paff, I thank you for freeing me from the persecutions of a *creature*, I will not say *man*, who to the crime of bigamy has added those of thief and burglar.

Craddock. So all this time you have been coaxing me into a trap?

O'Paff. That's about it brother Craddock.

Craddock. And you sir, [*To Sawyer.*] calling yourself a reputable member of the bar, accept my retainer, and then betray me into the hands of my enemies.

Sawyer. You're wrong again, Mr. Craddock. I did your work legitimately.

O'Paff. Exactly, but while he was looking up your estates, I was looking up your pedigree in the interest of my personal client. It was an accident, sir, pure and simple, by which this firm found itself retained upon two sides of one case You tried to inveigle us into a partnership in your rascality, but we thereby discovered that we had struck a gold mine in equity, and we determined to work it, for all it was worth.

Craddock Indeed! and what do you expect to accomplish by your double dealing? You have but the word of this woman, she is my wife, and the law shall yet compel her to submit to me.

Mrs. Montague. The day when that could happen has passed, thank heaven? I hold in my hand a certified copy of the registry of your marriage to Julia Green, a year before I, a thoughtless school girl, unfortunately met you at Bath.

O'Paff. If I were you, Mr. Craddock, I'd let the law alone, you don't seem to understand its complex ramifications. [CRADDOCK *with angry gesture starts to door* R.

Sir Randall. A word before you go. This lady, who has never been your wife, has from this day a lawful protection in Sir Randall Burns, a fact which you will do well to bear in mind.

O'Paff. Exactly, and if you are now permitted to go your way unmolested, you owe it to this noble lady, and her devoted friends, who prefer to see justice cheated, rather than have her pure name associated with yours in a public scandal.

Sawyer. [*Aside to* O'PAFF.] You're not going to let him go now?

O'Paff. [*Aside to* SAWYER.] I don't want to frighten him
yet, he'll not go far. [*Aloud.*] Good morning, Mr. Craddock, you'll find the stairway at the end of the hall, turn
left and you'll be right

CRADDOCK *moves to door* R. 2 E. O'PAFF *and* SAWYER *in*
act of bowing him out. CONTI. *on cue, appears in* C. D.,
he sees RITTA, *and makes gesture as though he would*
seize her. At same moment, HOFFMEIER *is at his side,*
and taps him on shoulder, he recoils. RITTA *sees* CONTI
and shrinks from him, SIR RANDALL *and* MRS. MONTA-
GUE *passing her over to* L. O'PAFF, SAWYER *and* CRAD-
DOCK, *do not see this action of the others, all of this is*
simultaneous and very quiet. PICTURE.

CLOSED IN.

SCENE 2D—*A modern street in first grooves.*

Enter KITTY L. 1 E., *she has on hat and shawl or coat, and*
is rather extravagantly dressed (loud colors, &c.).

Kitty Every Tuesday is my Sunday out. Well its a
most peculiar circumstance, but this is the first time Mr.
Hoffmeier was ever late in keeping an appointment. Oh!
but he's a foine man is Mr. Hoffmeier, and he's so fond of me,
and of cold chicken and beer. Faith I hardly know which he
likes the best. Oh, but he's a great man, is Mr. Hoffmeier,
and some of these foine days, he does be sayin,' he'll be a
Captain, or a Colonel, or an Alderman, or a Conductor, or
some great thing. I'll walk on down to the next corner,
maybe I'll catch him there on the beat. I wonder phat they
does be meanin' by the *bate?* Our butcher's boy says that
all of the policemen are on the bate. [*Exit* R. 1 E.
[*Enter* HOFFMEIER L. 1 E.

Hoffmeier. Dots what I call bad business, dot man ought
to have twenty years, and now after all we have done to run
him down, O'Paff lets him slip away just to save the voman
from scandal, maybe though he is only giving him a little
rope to let him hang himself. Any how I don't forgot dot
I must see O'Paff on important business at nine o'clock. I
vonder now what it can be about—I just had time to slip
down here and get my answer from Miss O'Rourke, I hope
she don't keep me waiting long. I vos bad gone on dot gal
sure. and de whole gang on de force giving me de grand
guy about it. [*Enter* KITTY *hurriedly* R. 1 E.

Kitty. Oho! you're there are ye?

Hoffmeier. Don't I look like I was here? I fly like Cupid on wings of love, to meet my red headed turtle-dove.

Kitty. Oh, Mr. Hoffmeier!

Hoffmeier. Call me Ferdinand. Have you brought me my answer? Can I get out the marriage license?

Kitty. Sure how do I know that you are not joking wid me, Mr. Hoffmeier?

Hoffmeier. Call me Ferdinand. No Miss O'Rourke, I don't joke on a serious business like getting married.

Kitty. Well, tell me phat's the reason that you don't marry a countryman of your own, Mr. Hoffmeier?

Hoffmeier. Call me Ferdinand.

Kitty. Well then Ferdinand, what's the reason that you want to marry a poor Irish girl like me?

Hoffmeier. All in the interest of harmony. If the whiskey vote and the beer vote is united we can sweep the whole country, and the American vote goes for nothing.

Kitty. Och, that's a great head you have on, Mr. Hoffmeier.

Hoffmeier. Call me Ferdinand.

Kitty. And you're quite sure that you love me, Mr. Hoffmeier?

Hoffmeier. Call me Ferdinand. Love you! why haven't I been telling you dot for two years? Do you think I was marrying for fun? No sir, when a Dutchman marries, he marries for business.

Kitty. Well, you'll not object to being married by the priest?

Hoffmeier. By the priest! no sir, ve got married at dot little protestant church around the corner.

Kitty. Oh, I couldn't, I couldn't, I couldn't.

Hoffmeier. We will make a compromise, and got married by the police justice, they see so much that they don't believe nothing.

Kitty Well I couldn't object to that. But you'll wait till after Christmas, won't ye?

Hoffmeier. Wait till after Christmas! Then maybe I will get left out in the cold.

Kitty. Well then you can come into my kitchen and warm.

Hoffmeier. Dot settles it. [*Embracing her and moving to* R. 1 E.] And the first boy will be called Ferdinand O'Rourke Hoffmeier!

Kitty. Oh, Mr. Hoffmeier!

Hoffmeier. Call me Ferdinand [*They exit* R. 1 E.
CHANGE OF SCENE.

SCENE 3D—*Same as Act 2d.*

Stage two-thirds dark, red lens through fire-place R., *throws red glare over the scene as a reflection from fire burning in grate.*

MUSIC. *As scene opens Old* ROSA *is discovered seated on floor in front of* L. *door leading under the stairway.* JIMMIE NIPPER *is at top of steps looking out door, as though on the lookout.* O'PAFF *is standing in front of grate.*

O'Paff. [*to* NIPPER.] Any signs of our man?

Jim. No, but I can see the Dutch cop Hoofmeir on the corner.

O'Paff. Tell him to come in, and then keep a sharp lookout for Conti.

Jim. Hall right. [*Exit* JIMMIE *upper door.*

O'Paff. [*To* ROSA.] And you are sure that Craddock and Conti are friends?

Rosa. Si, si padrone.

O'Paff. Does Craddock come here often?

Rosa. No, only two, tree times, always wid de beard to disguise de face.

O'Paff. Always in disguise, eh?

Rosa. Si padrone.

O'Paff. And once you heard them talk about a child? [ROSA *nods.*] Tell me again, what can you remember?

Rosa. Not a much. Conti watch a me all de time, he speak of London, fourteen year ago, a little child dat was lost. Rosa not a hear a plain. But dis much I hear, de fine gentleman in London, he give Conti money, de great money, to kill de child, and Conti swear to him dat de child was dead, and den he laugh and seem satisfy.

O'Paff. And Conti told Craddock that the child was dead?

Rosa. Si padrone.

O'Paff. It's as plain as day. Every link in the chain is complete. [HOFFMEIER *enters at upper door.*

O'Paff. Hoffmeier, where's your man?

Hoffmeier. He is working down this way. I've got one of the boys in citizens clothes shadowing him. What did you get out of the old woman?

[HOFFMEIER *is now down in room* L. C.

O'Paff. Enough to confirm my theory. Conti or Viotti

was hired to do away with the child, with the cunning instinct of his tribe, he has raised her as his own, intending when Craddock came into the estates to use the girls as a means of extorting hush money.

Hoffmeier. That looks very reasonable. Do you think you can trust the old woman?

O'Paff. Oh yes; her fear of punishment and her hatred of Conti make her a safe instrument in our hands.

Jim. [*Entering hurriedly.*] Old macaroni is comin. [*Exit* JIM.

Hoffmeier. Shall we nab him now?

O'Paff. Yes, we'll take him across the street, where I have a room guarded and everything prepared. Come, in with ye, quick, and remember the police whistle will be the signal for you.

O'Paff and Hoffmeier exit through door L. *under stairway. Rosa hu ries down and crouches down on floor in front of fire assorting rags.* [*Enter* CONTI, *carrying organ, he slams the door after him angrily.*

Conti. Damn a de lawyer! *He comes down and places organ on floor at back.* Damn a Ritta! *He sits sullenly on bench or stool* R. Damn a de Dutch policeman! me watch a Craddock, he see de lawyer too, he get de great property in England. Now was a my time, and now Ritta was a gone. Well all a de same, I can a frighten him, and make him give a me my share. [O'PAFF *comes out and moves to foot of stairs*] I find a him now and settle wid a' him. [*Starts up to steps and sees* O'PAFF.] PAUSE.

O'Paff. Good evening, Mr. Conti.

Conti. What you want a here?

O'Paff. Well as you declined to answer my questions, I thought I'd drop around and see whether you had changed your mind.

Conti. No, me got a noting to tell a you. You leave a my house.

O'Paff. I'm going Mr. Conti, and I'll trouble you to keep me company.

Conti. What a for me go wid a you?

O'Paff. Because I've taken fancy to your society.

Conti. Me not a go, a friend he come to see me, I must a wait.

O'Paff. You can see your friend to-morrow. Come brother Conti. [O'PAFF *moves up steps.*

Conti. Me not a go.

O'Paff. Oh yes ye will.

Conti. No! You make me trouble enough, you make a me no more. [*Whips out stilleto, at same moment* HOFF-MEIER *appears through door, and covers him with large revolver.*]

Hoffmeier. Dot's enough of dot nonsense now. Go ahead.

O'Paff. I thought you'd change your mind.

[CONTI *hangs back.*]

Hoffmeier. Come on now, go ahead.

O'PAFF *goes up stairs and off.* CONTI *is next followed by* HOFFMEIER *with revolver.* CONTI *turns two or three times, and* HOFFMEIER *shoves the pistol under his nose. As* CONTI *reaches door, he brandishes his knife with savage facial expression for the audience to see, conveying by action that he will stab* O'PAFF. *All off.* O'PAFF *makes rapid change to a double of* CONTI. MUSIC CHANGED. OLD ROSA *who has been watching the above action eagerly, stealthily runs over and looks into door under stairway, puts her finger to her lips as sign of silence to persons in the inner room, then stealthily goes up the stairs, and looks out onto street, laughs triumphantly, shaking her fist towards those outside as though gloating over a triumph. Comes down stairs laughing savagely (action to make time for* O'PAFF's *change .*

Rosa. [*At foot of stairs.*] Io lo detesto! (I hate him) Villano! Aha! Conti you treat a old Rosa like a slave! beat a her like a de dog. You put a your foot on a me like a de worm, some a time de worm will a sting a de foot of de tiger, and de savage beast will a die from de poison so you shall die from a de sting of de blow you give a me. Aha! Conti! Avro vendetta! Avro vendetta! (I will have revenge)

CRADDOCK *appears in door at top of steps, peers down into room, then closes door and comes down, he has on overcoat and beard worn in 2d Act.*

Craddock. [*on platform.*] This place is as dark as the devil's pit, and smells worse than usual, if such a thing were possible. [*Come down.*] Now what the devil can this Italian want with me? It must be somethiug important, or he would never run the risk of sending me a written message like this: [*Takes piece of dirty paper (crumpled) from his pocket and reads.*] " Must see you at my place to-night at just ten o'clock, don't fail this is a matter of great importance to both of us. Destroy this note when read. Don't fail, or you will long regret it. Conti." [*Lights his cigar with letter.*] I had forgotten that the fellow could write at all, but I remember now, he told me he had received quite a decent education at Rome in his youth. He certainly writes better English than he speaks, that's often the case however. [*Sees* ROSA.] Hello ! Is that you, Rosa ?

Rosa. Si padrone.

Craddock. [*Aside.*] The old hag ! She sends a cold chill down my back every time I look at her. [*Aloud.*] Where's Conti ?

Rosa. Conti go away.

Craddock. Gone away ! What the devil has he gone away for when he made an appointment with me for ten ? [*Looks at watch.*] It only wants five minutes now.

Rosa. Maybe Conti come back.

Craddock. I dare say he will. Leave the room, d'ye hear !

Rosa Si signore. Rosa hear. [*xes to door under stairs.*] [*Aside.*] Rosa hear, more dan Rosa shall a hear, more dan Rosa shall a hear. [*Exit under stairway closing door.*]

Craddock. I wonder where Conti dug that old mummy up, and what he keeps her about for ? [*Taking off overcoat and beard.*] I dare say he makes her useful in some way, he wouldn't have her around if he couldn't. Matters are beginning to look rather squally for me, what cursed fatality ever led me to the office of that firm ? I was an impatient fool anyway. I should have concealed my identity till the expiration of my term, then gone quietly to London and established my claim. I should then have had money enough to pave my way to safety, and to buy the silence of idle pratlers, and it all comes of that woman, curse her ! and I loved her too, or at least I came as near to it as I could to loving anything but myself. At this moment, I'm completely at the mercy of those fellows, my only safety is their desire to avoid a public scandal. The sword of Damocles is suspended above my neck on the thread of a woman's caprice, altogether too slight a support for my peace of mind. I'm a spotted man from this day and the sooner I disappear the better. I'll slip over to San Francisco, live quietly, and let this affair blow over before I make another attempt. Where the deuce can that Italian be ?

MUSIC. *Distant clock commences striking ten,* CRADDOCK *takes out his watch, on last stroke of ten, the door is thrown open, and* O'PAFF *disguised, as* CONTI *enters hurriedly, closing and apparently locking the door behind him, he has* CONTI'S *knife in his hand, the idea to convey to the audience is that* CONTI *has killed his captors and escaped.*

Craddock. [*After* CONTI *closes door.*] Prompt to the minute. O'PAFF *knife in hand hurries down the steps looking back as though fearful of being pursued.* CRADDOCK *is seated on corner of table* R.

Craddock. Oh you're here are you! Why weren't you here to meet me? What's the matter with you?

O'Paff. [*Imitating voice and manner of* CONTI.] Matter enough wid a me, me say ten a de clock, de clock strike a ten, me a here.

Craddock. Well now that you are here, what do you want, and why didn't you take some other means of communicating with me, instead of sending a dirty gamin with a dirtier piece of paper into a public hotel to be seen talking to a gentleman.

O'Paff. Gentleman! Bah! You make a me sick.

Craddock. Yes, you Italian dog, a gentleman. Well what is it? Out with it.

O'Paff. De *gentleman* is in a bad a temper a to-night.

Craddock. Possibly I am. I've had enough to put me in a bad temper, and I want no more irritation to make me worse. Come what do you want?

O'Paff. I want to settle de old score. I want a my share.

Craddock. Old score! Your share! Share of what?

O'Paff. Oh, you know what I mean.

Craddock. Haven't I always kept my word with you, and gone snacks in everything we worked together.

O'Paff. No, not all a de time.

Craddock. What job have I failed to divy on?

O'Paff. De great job of all, de property in England.

Craddock. The property in England?

O'Paff. Si, you was a to see de lawyer.

Craddock. Well, what then?

O'Paff. I was to see de lawyer too, I want a my share.

Craddock. Your share of what?

O'Paff. You know, you know, my share of your fader's property.

Craddock. Why, you fool ! I haven't got it yet, and possibly I never shall, besides I paid you all you asked for what you did, you would not dare turn traitor.

O'Paff. Call a me what a you like, so long I get a my share.

Craddock. See here, Viotti—

O'Paff. What for you call a me, Viotti ?

Craddock. Well, its your name, isn't it

O'Paff. No, not a here.

Craddock. It's your name to *me* at all times. And I've paid you like a prince for every service you have done me. If this is what you got me here for, you might have saved yourself the trouble. Your road and mine lie in different directions hereafter. Stand aside. [CRADDOCK *moves to* C.

O'Paff. Stop ! you shall not a go till you sign a de paper to give five tousand dollar, on a demand.

Craddock. You're a fool ! How can I give what I haven't got?

O'Paff. It is a lie.

Craddock. [*Moving hand towards pistol pocket.*] What !

O'Paff. Yes, a lie. [*On picture with knife.*] I wait a for you to come a back for fourteen year ; you tink now I let a you go wid everyting after I wait for you so long.

Craddock. So you threaten, do you? You miserable traitor ! I might have known better than to trust one of your accursed tribe. But what can you say or do?

O'Paff. What can I do ? Everyting. I can a denounce you to de authorities as de abductor of your a sister's child.

Craddock. And I can denounce you as her murderer.

O'Paff. Well, do ! and we go hand in hand to de scaffold, hand in hand to hell. See who will a be de first a one to cry.

Craddock. [*Trying to pass up* C.] Stand out of my path, you Italian dog.

O'Paff. You refuse a to share wid me

Craddock. I refuse to talk to you until you come to your senses, stand aside.

O'Paff. Stop !

Craddock. Out of my way !

O'Paff. Stop ! [*Savagely branding his knife.*] Hear a me one word more, den you can go. [*Points to paper &c., on table.*] Dere is de paper, dere is de pen. Write on de paper dot so soon you get your fader's property, you give to Paulo Viotti, five tousand pound, for service done to you. Den sign a your name.

Craddock. Why, you're mad.

O'Paff. You refuse to write.

Craddock. Yes.

O'Paff. Den your fate on your own head. Dis night I seek a de friend of de child. Dey will give a me de mon when I give a back de child.

Craddock. [*In alarm.*] Give back the child ! what child ?

O'Paff. Oh, you know what a child.

Craddock. You miserable traitor ! do you dare to tell me that my sister's child is living ! that you did not kill her as you swore to me that you had done.

O'Paff. What for I kill a de child, when she worth a more to me alive.

Craddock. Where is she now ?

O'Paff. Dat's for me, not for you to know.

Craddock. I remember now, Jim told me of a girl you had used on the street, but the law took her away from you.

O'Paff. Si, de law take her beyond the reach of my hand, but not beyond the reach of my tongue, when it speak a de truth.

Craddock. Bah ! it's a lie—it is one of your own accursed tribe, a partner in a plot in which you hope to frighten me. I can denounce you both as a pair of imposters, and who would credit the denial of a spotted criminal such as you.

O'Paff. You tink no one believe a me ?

Craddock. No.

O'Paff. May be so. But dey will believe dere own eyes, when dey see de mark on de body of de child, which she carry from her infancy.

Craddock. [*Starting aside.*] The burn upon the shoulder ?

O'Paff. Si—aha ? de burn on a de shoulder, you rememb ? De burn on de shoulder—it is a describe to day on de record of de London police.

Craddock. [*Aside rapidly.*] I am at his mercy—oh why did I not kill the brat myself.

O'Paff. Now you will write a de paper ?

Craddock. First answer me a question. Does the girl know the truth.

O'Paff. No, de secret is wid a me, and wid a you alone.

Craddock. You swear it ?

O'Paff. I swear it.

Craddock. [*Aside.*] Then my course is clear.

O'Paff. Now you will write a de paper ?

Craddock. [*Appearing to yield.*] Oh, I've no objection.

Craddock moves up to table, as though to sit down, and so gets between O'Paff and the stairway.

O'Paff. Who is de master now?

Craddock. [*Jumping to foot of stairs and drawing large size nickel-plated pocket-pistol*] I am, you double dyed traitor. [PICTURE. O'PAFF *shrinks.*

O'Paff. What would a you do?

Craddock. What does the stag do when the hound brings him to bay? He kills, as I'll kill you.

O'Paff. You would not dare to murder me.

Craddock. Why should I not?

O'Paff. Because you are a coward, and you dare not face de hangman.

Craddock. Bah—the character of this den is known. I will say that you decoyed me here to rob me, and that I shot you in self-defense—the knife in your hand will convict you, and dead men make no denials.

O'Paff. Stop! I will leave a de country and trouble you no more.

Craddock. [*Moving up steps.*] No, I've trusted you once too often. This world is not large enough for both of us. You have sworn the secret was with us two—when you are dead, it will be with me alone.

During speech he approaches top of steps, so timing the action that he reaches the door on the last word, the pistol covering O'PAFF *as he ascends. On the words " me alone," O'PAFF blows police whistle—the door is thrown open and* CONTI *stands face to face with* CRADDOCK. HOFFMEIER *behind—strong calcium thrown on the picture, as though it was the moon, coming in through the open door—*CRADDOCK *staggers back aghast—* PICTURE. *After picture* CRADDOCK *backs down the steps, looking wildly at* CONTI, *then at* O'PAFF. CONTI *and* HOFFMEIER *follow down steps—they all drop down* R. CONTI *sees* O'PAFF, *stares at him in utter bewilderment.* O'PAFF *quietly removes his disguise as the calcium is thrown upon the group.*

Craddock [*Aside.*] Fool, blind fool and dupe that I have been.

O'Paff. I quite agree with you, Mr. Craddock, although the remark is not complimentary to my skill as a detective.

Hoffmeier. [*Covering Craddock with revolver.*] Put down that gun.

CRADDOCK *sullenly places his pistol on table.* HOFFMEIER *picks it up, puts it in his pocket.*

Craddock. Your plot was a very clever one, but you forgot one important adjunct.

O'Paff. And what was that?

Craddock. Witnesses! All men are equal before the law, and my oath will weigh against your own. [*Lights all up.*

RITTA *enters from door under stairs followed by* MRS. MONTAGUE, SIR RANDALL *and* ROSA, *who brings on a lamp.*

Ritta. But not against ours, Jasper Craddock! We have heard you convict yourself by your own confession.

Craddock. A very clever trick, sir, but it is before the Courts of England, that these charges are to be answered, and you have no authority to bar my passage from this room.

SAWYER *and* JOE SKERRETT, *an English detective officer, enter onto platform and at once descend steps.* JIMMIE NIPPER *on, remains on platform.*

Sawyer. You're wrong again brother Craddock, allow me to introduce you to Joseph Skerrett, Esquire, special agent of the London detective police, Scotland Yards. Skerrett, Craddock; Craddock,.Skerrett,

Skerrett. Train a little late, but I got here on time. [*Produces legal documents.*] The extradition papers for Jasper Craddock and Paulo Viotto, duly signed by *the* Secretary of State.

Happy to meet you gentlemen, after so many years. Why I should have known either of you, among a thousand.

[*Assists* HOFFMEIER *to put the double handcuffs on* CRADDOCK *and* CONTI.]

Craddock. Well, Conti, there's a consolation in knowing that *you did not betray me.*

Conti. [*Half aside.*] I didn't get a de chance.

O'Paff. [*To* RITTA.] You thought my plan a desperate one, dear, you see that I was right.

Ritta. You are always right, Felix, as you were when you first saw beneath my sun-burned face a something that told you I was not what I seemed to be.

O'Paff. It was a sacred instinct, dear, and no credit to myself. An All-Wise Providence made the poor, briefless lawyer his humble instrument.

Sir Randall. O'Paff, old boy, this case is a fortune to you
if you never win another.

SIR RANDALL *and* HELEN L., O'PAFF *and* RITTA C., SAW-
YER R. C., CONTI, CRADDOCK, HOFFMEIER *and* SKERRET
R., *a little in background.* OLD ROSA, *holding lamp a*
back, L.

Ritta. [*To* O'PAFF.] You have won your case and clien
too.

Sawyer. On a brief without a flaw.

Mrs. Montague. [*To* SIR RANDALL.] You've been mos
loyal in your love.

O'Paff. And now we're all sound in Law.

MUSIC. O'PAFF *embraces* RITTA, SIR RANDALL *embrace*
HELEN, SAWYER *slaps his hat down on the floor, rams hi*
hands in his pockets, and walks up stage in disgust. JIM-
MIE *dancing.* KITTY *follows* JIMMIE *on at end, an*
remains on platform. They embrace as curtain descend
HOFFMEIER *tries to get at them and is restrained by* SAW-
YER.

CURTAIN.

www.ingramcontent.com/pod-product-compliance
Lightning Source LLC
Chambersburg PA
CBHW030005030726
47499CB00008B/2911